The PIRATES of TURTLE ROCK

The PIRATES of TURTLE ROCK

Richard W. Jennings

 Houghton Mifflin Company

Boston 2008

All rights reserved. For information about permission to
reproduce selections from this book, write to Permissions,
Houghton Mifflin Company, 215 Park Avenue South,
New York, New York 10003.

www.houghtonmifflinbooks.com

The text of this book is set in New Century Schoolbook.

Library of Congress Cataloging-in-Publication Data

Jennings, Richard W. (Richard Walker), 1945-
The pirates of Turtle Rock / by Richard W. Jennings.
p. cm.
"This story originally appeared in somewhat different form in thirty-seven
weekly installments from December 3, 2006, to August 12, 2007, in Star
Magazine, the Sunday magazine of The Kansas City Star,
Tim Janicke, editor."
Summary: Sixteen-year-old Jenny Snow of South Florida finds
the adventurous life she craves when she joins forces with
eighteen-year-old Coop DeVille, a seventh-generation pirate,
to seek the lost turtle totem of the Ugiri-Tom.
ISBN-13: 978-0-618-98793-1
ISBN-10: 0-618-98793-2
[1. Pirates—Fiction. 2. Buried treasure—Fiction. 3. Adventure and
adventurers—Fiction. 4. Florida— Fiction. 5. Caribbean Area—Fiction. 6.
Humorous stories.] I. Title.
PZ7.J42007085Pir 2008
[Fic]—dc22

2008000763

Printed in the United States of America
MP 10 9 8 7 6 5 4 3 2 1

TO WALTER LORRAINE

Keeper of the Flame

ACKNOWLEDGMENTS

This story originally appeared in thirty-seven weekly install-ments in *Star Magazine* from December 3, 2006, to August 12, 2007. The Sunday magazine of the *Kansas City Star* is edited by Tim Janicke.

One chapter was published in a modified form as "Mr. Potter's Patio Garden," in the July 2007 issue of the *Best Times*, Lynn Anderson, editor.

This full-length, hardcover volume contains abundant new material and substantial revisions. It was edited for the Houghton Mifflin Company, Boston and New York, by Stacy Graham O'Connell.

To each I extend my thanks for your kindness, your patience, your support, and your skilled counsel.

R.W.J.
Overland Park, Kansas
2008

THE GOD OF THE UGIRI-TOM

IN THE WARM WATERS of the Caribbean lies a tiny island—little more than an atoll, really—that for centuries remained undiscovered and untouched by all but a small group of natives who lived on larger islands nearby.

Calling themselves the Ugiri-Tom, these gentle people worshiped the sea and the myriad forms of life within.

Among the Ugiri-Tom, no creature was more revered than the great loggerhead turtle (*Caretta caretta*), which the Ugiri-Tom called *ageri gop aquera*—"winged god of the sea."

Believing the uninhabited spit of coral, salt, scrub palmetto, and sand to be the sea turtle's place of origin, the Ugiri-Tom considered this to be the most sacred spot in the universe.

Each night before sunset, a band of men and women made up of the Ugiri-Tom's most worthy members set out in outrigger canoes to protect their sea-god's hallowed birthplace from being swallowed up by the ocean like the sun.

Over the course of many years, these holy night watchmen erected a temple to their god, in front of which they placed a totem that soared to a height three times that of the average Ugiri-Tom—nearly seventeen feet.

Not having the gold or silver or precious stones possessed by other civilizations of their era, the Ugiri-Tom meticulously crafted their great loggerhead turtle likeness from the abundant natural pearl that lined the shells of the rich array of indigenous bivalves.

How it glistened in the bright Caribbean sun!

For generations, the Ugiri-Tom lived in harmony with nature and at peace among themselves, practicing the teachings of their sea-god by day and protecting its fragile home after darkness, until one terrifying night in 1795, when, under a full moon, summoned by the shimmering, pearlescent, turtle-shaped beacon, pirates arrived.

During the futile defense that ensued, two brave Ugiri-Tom brothers, identical twins named Tak-Me and Tak-Ma, hurriedly lashed their outriggers together, then secured the sacred statue across the canoes and set out for parts unknown.

Deprived of treasure, the pirates punished the Ugiri-Tom in the only way that pirates know, and thus, the history of these quiet, isolated people sadly ended.

But what of the two brothers? What became of them? And what, we wonder, even today, of their magnificent totem?

A VERY PRIVATE PLACE

ON THE ATLANTIC COAST of South Florida, in a town called Kansas-by-the-Sea, there is a short stretch of shoreline where the rocky reef comes right up to the sand. Here waves crash and send salt spray into the air. In certain places, the sea has carved out blowholes, much like the exhaust vents of whales, and when the tide and wind are right, water spouts through these openings like geysers.

Except for the occasional presence of raucous sea birds responding opportunistically to a quick meal, this is a quiet spot, hidden behind a canopy of sea grapes and fenced by clumps of tall, brittle grasses. It is a place largely unvisited by tourists and sunbathers, who prefer the more accessible beaches a couple of miles to the south. The ones with restaurants and parking lots and margarita bars nearby.

While real estate developers and their banker pals have done their best to cover every square foot of unstable South Florida beachfront with a vacation home or retirement condominium, the forty acres of this particular place are owned by a perpetual conservation trust, making it legally off-limits to construction of any kind.

Sharks live in these waters. Jellyfish. Manta rays. Fish of every size and kind. And, of course, the rare and endangered loggerhead turtle. The only boats allowed near the shore are operated by the United States Coast Guard to warn away pleasure craft and to arrest any fishermen they encounter.

At least once every season, and oftentimes more, hurricanes pass through this region to rearrange the looks of the place.

But one object never changes.

One very large chunk of the reef lies halfway in the water, halfway on the beach, a massive rock roughly the size of a Waste Management Corporation trash-collecting truck.

Over the years, the rock has been broken into two nearly equal pieces by the relentless pounding of the mighty forces of nature, or so the locals believe, since none can recall a time when the rock wasn't broken.

They call this fractured formation Turtle Rock.

Turtle Rock is where sixteen-year-old Jennifer Snow comes to sit and listen to her iPod and think about the tedium that is her life.

Today, Jenny's hair is brown. Last week it was red. A month before, it was blond. If variations in hair color are any indication of a person's state of mind, Jenny Snow is a girl in search of an identity.

She is also a person who, inch by inch, and thought by thought, is running away from home, whether she realizes it or not.

Jenny's mother and father are well-meaning but infinitely boring people, who, because they seem to have nothing to say to each other, to Jenny's way of thinking, never should have gotten together in the first place, and certainly, when they

4

did, never should have decided to have a child, since after they had one they achieved nothing of any consequence since.

Although the temperature is an ideal seventy-two degrees Fahrenheit (twenty-two degrees Celsius), the only other people in the vicinity are a pair of young lovers who've stationed themselves about a hundred yards down the beach, partially protected from view by an overhang of reef rock made possible by low tide. At first Jenny tries to ignore them, but their presence eventually causes her to wonder about her own relationship.

Jenny has a boyfriend of sorts, a fifteen-year-old admirer named Burson whose awkward attentions Jenny finds mildly flattering, but Burson hasn't exactly followed up on his opportunity. Perhaps his writing her name on his notebook in red Magic Marker surrounded by a border of concentric hearts has embarrassed her.

With love, you never know.

The music bounces and throbs in Jenny's ears. The sea performs its liquid ballet. From this distance, the lovers down the beach seem a single entity.

Jenny bites her fingernails.

If Jenny were not so preoccupied, or were focusing on the breakers colliding against the expansive reef rather than listening to music, or were looking out to sea instead of staring at the indistinct couple half hidden in the shadows, she might notice the object looming on the horizon. But as it is, Jenny is paying no more attention to it than she is to the passing clouds.

This is unwise.

Because on board that ship, someone is definitely paying attention to her.

THE REPREHENSIBLE

EVEN THOUGH THEY are commonly found in the company of others, pirates do not have friends.

Certainly not best friends.

Have you ever seen a "buddy movie" about pirates?

There's a reason for that.

Captain Cooper "Coop" DeVille has been at sea for more than six months. Six months without a soul to talk to but his crew, whom he dislikes intensely. So, naturally, he is in a terrible mood. For a career pirate, even one who's only eighteen years old, this is a serious condition.

As is well known, pirates are capable of the most despicable behavior, seemingly without provocation. For Coop DeVille, six months at sea verged on serious provocation.

DeVille summoned his first mate, an elderly man and formerly fashionable English butler named Henry.

"Henry," DeVille demanded in a surly tone of voice, "fetch me my spyglass."

"Right away, Captain," his servant replied, sloping his shoulders forward and bowing his head slightly as he scurried to Captain DeVille's stateroom.

Within minutes, the restless DeVille had his sights set on a supine Jenny Snow sunning herself on Turtle Rock. He marveled at her fresh, unspoiled beauty. He also noted the remoteness of her surroundings.

"Ah!" DeVille announced to Henry. "This day may yet turn out to provide an entry for the logbook. Quickly, lower the dinghy."

"Shall I assemble a landing party, Captain?" the obedient Henry asked.

"Did I command you to assemble a landing party?" DeVille responded petulantly.

"No, sir, you did not," Henry answered.

"Then don't presume to do my thinking for me," DeVille snapped at his servant.

"As you wish," Henry replied.

Cooper hated it when other people assumed they knew what was on his mind. What could the fawning Henry know of the attractions of mermaids on the rocks? All Coop desired was some quiet time spent in this water sprite's company, and perhaps the exchange of a story, or the gift of a song or two.

And would a kiss—just a light but promising grazing of the lips—be entirely out of the question?

Coop DeVille was a seventh-generation pirate. His father, his grandfather, his great-grandfather, and so on all had been pirates before him, sailing virtually unchallenged throughout the Caribbean, where they took whatever they wanted whenever the opportunity presented itself.

This is why some people find the field of piracy so appealing—namely, everything is free—but let me suggest that your teachers, librarians, law enforcement officials, and religious leaders, as well as your parents, will advise you to consider a different career altogether. It would be a good idea to listen to them.

Now to return to the story.

The ship itself, a three-masted square-rigger outfitted with twenty-four guns and a crew of equal number, is capable of remaining at sea for a year or more, so long as the pickings are good, and in the warm blue-green waters of the Caribbean, the pickings, consisting primarily of wealthy elderly tourists from the Midwest enjoying their first cruise, are excellent.

The pirate ship had been lovingly handed down from generation to generation, from Blackbeard, to Whitebeard, to Brownbeard, to Redbeard, to Graybeard, to Auburn-with-blond-highlights-Beard, to the clean-shaven Cooper, with repairs and ship-improvement projects performed along the way.

Called the *Reprehensible,* the ship caused all who encountered it to decry their luck, if they lived long enough.

In certain official quarters of the governments of various nations and island states, the *Reprehensible* had taken on the cache of legend. In fact, many now believed the ship existed only in the imaginations of a few gullible Minnesotans, from which there are a great many to choose.

So far as the authorities were concerned, the *Reprehensible* was no more real than the Ghost Ship of Captain "Peach" Daiquiri, the Giant Squid of the Sargasso Sea, or Satan's Screaming Seaplane from the Skies.

This suited Coop DeVille just fine.

Out of mind, out of sight, out of danger, he thinks.

In the dinghy, DeVille begins rowing toward his innocent, unwary quarry. Years of literally whipping recalcitrant crew members into submission have built up his biceps to the point at which his muscular arms are capable of powering the dinghy for hours.

As has been noted, pirates enjoy abundant freedom.

But pirates are subject to many of the same confluences of circumstance that affect the rest of us.

For example, there is an invisible but well-established line between desire and opportunity in which fate most enjoys demonstrating her infinite superiority to man. This is the main reason one should never tempt fate.

Fate is a sucker for temptation.

In this case, fate's messenger is a junior officer in the United States Coast Guard, a new enlistee named Paul Afton Wright, a youth no older than DeVille, who, brandishing an unloaded but menacing-looking pistol, waves DeVille away from the reef.

"You're boating in a protected area," he explains. "Turn back!"

"Argh!" responds DeVille, reluctantly turning his craft around.

Meanwhile, oblivious to the encounter taking place just out of earshot, Jenny Snow picks up her belongings and follows the cool sandy path through the sea grape bower to where she parked her blue Vespa.

Curses! thinks DeVille.

HOME SWEET HOME

HALFWAY BETWEEN TURTLE ROCK and Jenny Snow's South Florida townhouse stands a red lighthouse that can be seen for miles. Although it no longer serves to guide ships from the stormy Atlantic into the safety of the inlet at Kansas-by-the-Sea, it remains the singular physical feature of the region— quite literally Kansas-by-the-Sea's landmark.

As far as Jenny is concerned, while she finds the lighthouse to be pretty in a nautical sort of way, it is simply one of those things that has always been and always will be. Since she has never lived anywhere else, it has not occurred to her that such a structure is any more special than a row of white-painted grain elevators beside the railroad tracks in Kansas City, or a faded wooden barn on a hillside in Bowling Green, Kentucky.

Coop DeVille, however, teenage pirate, makes a lengthy notation that evening about the position of the lighthouse in his ship's log.

"She'll be back," Deville announces to his parrot, a philosophical African gray male named Ruthless, "and so will I."

"Maybe," Ruthless observes in that enigmatic way parrots have of expressing themselves, an affectation that more than any other has thwarted scientists' efforts to establish meaningful interspecies communication with the clever creatures.

"Oh, what do you know?" DeVille responds.

"Oh, what do you know?" repeats Ruthless.

Meanwhile, Jenny parks her Vespa in the garage just as her father is returning from his job in West Palm Beach, where he is managing editor of *Corrections* magazine.

From its name, you might think *Corrections* has something to do with the nation's burgeoning prison industry, but this is not the case. Instead, *Corrections* is a weekly newsmagazine with the mission of correcting mistakes in the items it published the week before. It is a very thick magazine, packed with advertisements from luxury automobile dealers, divorce lawyers, orthodontists, plastic surgeons, real estate developers, and a unique service for flash-freezing the recently departed called Last Chance for a Second Chance.

Although it assures him a steady paycheck, Jenny's father dislikes his job.

"I never feel like I'm making any progress," he complains over a frozen lasagna dinner thawed by Jenny's mother, an elementary school art teacher. "Just once, I'd like to get caught up."

"I know what you mean," his wife replies. "Today the entire panda poster display came unstuck from the hall walls. What a mess! I think I may need bigger glue guns."

Jenny Snow rolls her eyes at her parents' banal conversation while she concentrates on finishing the food on her plate.

"What did you do today, honey?" her mother asks.

"The same thing I do every day," Jenny replies sullenly. "Nothing."

Jenny picks up her dishes, rinses them in the sink, and goes to her room, where she clicks on her TV.

A pirate movie is on.

She watches it without interest, observing that it consists primarily of cutlass fights, cannon fire, and scruffy-looking men in tattered, fancy costumes, saying "Argh!"

All of them look as if they could use a shower.

Once in a while someone buries treasure in the sand, typically gold coins in a wooden chest, but sometimes diamonds, emeralds, rubies, and pearls. Later, someone else digs it up, only to set off another series of fights, grimaces, curses, spitting, and "arghs."

After half an hour, Jenny changes the channel to a home shopping show. Ironically, it too is about gold jewelry and its timeless allure.

Except for her mother's wedding ring, the only precious object in Jenny's house is an antique locket handed down to her mother by a great-grandmother, who got it from an even greater-grandmother, and beyond that everyone living has lost track of its origin. Jenny's mother presented it to Jenny on the day she turned sixteen.

Jenny has never worn the locket because she is saving it for a special occasion, and, as has been pointed out, the total absence of special occasions in Jenny Snow's life is at the root of her unhappiness. Also, although the locket is framed in an intricate gold filigree that looks as if it were spun by fairies, within its secret compartment it contains a dark wispy coil of human hair, a relic Jenny finds to be as disgusting as gallstones preserved in a bottle.

As to whom the hair had once belonged, no one seems to

know, but it is presumed to be that of a family member from the distant past, or possibly, as Jenny prefers to imagine, that of a distant relative's lover.

That night, as Jenny falls asleep, she clasps the locket in her hand and makes a wish.

She does not wish for riches, as so many do, or for health, for which so many must, and neither does she wish for love, as so many cry out whose hearts have recently been broken. No, what Jenny Snow wishes for that night is danger, because in her mind danger is the only thing that can break this endless siege of boredom.

THE NIGHT VISITOR

IN THE MIDDLE OF THE NIGHT, Jenny Snow awakens suddenly with the sensation that something is amiss. As most people do when they suspect nocturnal intruders, she lies perfectly still and listens intently, hoping that she is mistaken. What she hears, however, is not encouraging—something nearby is either sifting flour or ruffling feathers.

Either there is a baker at work in my room, or I am at the mercy of invading owls, Jenny concludes.

Either way, given the circumstances, it is a disquieting thought.

And then it speaks.

"State name," the voice demands.

The startling words sound as if they have been prerecorded and are now being played back through a drive-thru restaurant speaker. Certainly what Jenny hears is not a live human voice. This increases her consternation.

"State name," the voice repeats.

"Florida," Jenny responds. "The name of the state is Florida."

"No, no, no," the voice says. "*Your* name."

"Yeah, okay," Jenny says bravely while fumbling under the bed for a baseball bat or fireplace poker, if not a lead pipe, candlestick holder, rope, or pipe wrench, none of which, alas, seem to be at hand. "But you go first."

"Awk!" screeches the voice.

"Well, what is it?" Jenny demands.

"What's what?" the voice responds.

"Your name, birdbrain!" Jenny shouts in exasperation.

"Ruthless," comes the reply.

"Ruthless," Jenny repeats.

"Ruthless," the voice confirms.

"Anybody ever call you Ruth?" she asks.

"Never twice," the voice answers menacingly.

Jenny switches on the lamp beside her bed. The sudden illumination reveals a large bird, but not so big as your basic frying chicken. It is a parrot of a variety known as African gray, a handsome bird with a brilliant brush of red on its otherwise gray flannel suit.

"Awk!" screeches Ruthless.

"Well, aren't you a pretty one," Jenny observes.

"Likewise," Ruthless replies.

"Many thanks," Jenny says. "Now get out of my room."

"Your name," Ruthless repeats.

Sighing, Jenny answers, "It's Jennifer. Now beat it."

With that, the parrot flies through the open bedroom window, repeating to itself, "Jennifer Nowbeatit, Jennifer Nowbeatit, Jennifer Nowbeatit."

There is nothing particularly unusual about a parrot in South Florida. Once, this lush, steamy subtropical peninsula was thick with the beating wings of countless numbers of the spectacular talking birds.

Modern development and the cultivation of sugar cane put an end to that, but in recent years small flocks of non-native parrots have begun assembling in the tall, decorative, non-native palm trees, a population started by old ladies who having acquired a parrot as a pet, soon tire of their companion's noisy and unhygienic shenanigans.

In any event, whether you like it or not, in South Florida, they're all over the place.

Thus, Jenny Snow does not consider her midnight visitor to be all that strange—no more than if a spider or mouse or scorpion or lizard or fat buffo toad or even an armadillo had crawled into her room insisting that she cough up her name or suffer the consequences.

Noteworthy, certainly, but in Jenny's view, not wholly out of the realm of reason.

When she wakes the next morning, she has already put the visitor out of her thoughts, concentrating instead on the toaster waffles that her mother has set out for Jenny to gobble down before mounting her Vespa for school.

If the preceding paragraph were to appear in *Corrections* magazine, the following paragraph, or something very much like it, would show up in subsequent weeks.

To be precise, Jenny's vehicle isn't truly a Vespa. It is a Piaggio Typhoon SE, made at the Vespa factory in Italy but significantly lower in price than a full-blown Vespa.

Jenny's parents are people of modest means.

That's okay, Jenny thinks. *Made at the Vespa factory is close enough.*

Besides, this near-Vespa suits Jenny nicely. As blue as the Atlantic Ocean sparkling in the sun, and equipped with a fifty-cubic-centimeter two-stroke gasoline engine more powerful than that of many popular lawn mowers, it allows Jenny, a daredevil driver, to dart in and out of traffic on Indiantown Road and be at Turtle Rock on Kansas-by-the-Sea Island in less than fifteen minutes.

Had it not been for this mobility, Jenny is quite certain that she would long ago have died from her life's meaningless monotony.

Change, however, is in the wind, and it is no mere ocean breeze.

As Jenny lies sunning herself upon the fractured landmark called Turtle Rock, the teenage pirate Coop DeVille fixes his spyglass on the object that chance (or fate) has placed before him, declaring, "Now hear this, Miss Nowbeatit, I am not setting sail without you."

Of all the differences that set the peoples of the world apart, none is so clear a divide as that which separates the wanderers from those with a rooted sense of place. Destiny has determined that some of us become nomads and sailors while the rest settle into being resolute nest makers.

There is no in between.

An apt metaphor for this separation is Turtle Rock. Cleft by forces not yet understood, the great boulder lies half in swirling water, half on land.

Jenny Snow is sitting on the upper half of the rock eating a bologna sandwich when a swimmer, breathing heavily, attempts to climb the lower half. Clenched between his teeth is a letter opener, an anniversary gift from Henry, which he hopes to pass off as a dagger in the event of trouble.

For all his history of derring-do, Coop DeVille continues to make a number of strategic errors.

Among them: After swimming all the way from ship to

pounding shore, he finds himself too tired to pull himself onto an object that rises twelve feet above his head; second, while it is theoretically possible to speak with a knifelike object in one's closed mouth, his words come out like those of an amateur attempting the art of ventriloquism, specifically, the well-known drinking-a-glass-of-water-while-the-dummy-talks trick.

"Mmf!" Deville says from the base of Turtle Rock. "Mmf, mm, maumpa glug!"

This, of course, is no way to begin a conversation.

With his weapon in his mouth and his body mostly submerged, Coop DeVille's unintelligible demand is delivered as waves crash noisily over the young pirate's waterlogged head.

Jenny, dark faux-designer glasses shielding her eyes, tiny earbuds inserted in her ears, is caught up in the mournful music of her favorite band, French Asparagus, so naturally she fails to notice the desperate Coop DeVille's entreaties.

"Mmf!" the teenage pirate repeats as a wave crashes against Turtle Rock, sending a spume spouting through a blowhole, which, in turn, causes Jenny Snow to abandon her post.

The tide must be coming in, she concludes.

Jenny gathers up her towel and picnic basket and tosses the remnants of her bologna sandwich into the sea, where it is promptly consumed by unseen living forces.

Meat deliberately thrown into the ocean is what fishermen call chum. Chum attracts meat-eating fish so the fishermen don't have to bother to search for them. In this case, all-beef bologna is a favorite food of sand sharks, small but athletic creatures that typically don't eat people whole, as great white sharks are known to do, but nevertheless are not averse to sampling what's available.

This has been known to include an ankle or two.

Think of sand sharks as the Yorkshire terriers of the sea.

Jenny Snow is already on her bright blue Vespa and passing the crowded Wendy's drive-through on Indiantown Road when a soggy Coop DeVille feels a nudge against his calf. Deftly responding with a plunge of his letter opener, DeVille is able to save himself from permanent disability or worse, after which, he lies on his back on the beach, exhausted, planning his next move.

People think pirates have it made, he thinks. *But what do they know?*

On board the *Reprehensible,* the crew is watching movies and playing video games recently liberated from a Blockbuster store in Vero Beach. It isn't the same as tallying up a treasure of precious jewels and Spanish gold, but it helps to pass the time until the distracted captain returns to business.

Pirates, of course, are thieves, but thieves of a particular sort. In their own minds, pirates are head and shoulders above catburglars, second-story men, pickpockets, kidnappers, lawn art robbers, short-change artists, carnival operators, advertising executives, stockbrokers, tax cheats, carwreck scammers, shoplifters, shakedown artists, door-to-door salesmen, counterfeiters, real estate speculators, tobacco lawyers, supplemental insurance salesmen, mortgage brokers, and carjackers, and should not even be compared to those to who pass poorly worded notes to bank tellers or point pistols at recently immigrated clerks in twenty-four-hour convenience stores.

In the hierarchy of the world's crooks, pirates believe themselves to be at the top. This, of course, reveals their ignorance of world politics, but no one has ever accused pirates of being educated people.

In fact, of the twenty-four crew members aboard the *Reprehensible,* only Henry, Captain DeVille's first mate and personal attendant, knows how to read. The rest are a ragtag pack of scalawags and misfits raised on a diet of electronic entertainment.

Yet even the lowest among these lowlifes considers himself to be a superior human being. This is largely due to the fact that pirates exert control not over the world's cities, with their newspapers, sports magazines, and libraries to contend with, but across its vast, borderless seas, where not so much as a single street sign or billboard stands in need of deciphering.

With a vocabulary limited to such words as "Argh," "Avast," "Yo-ho," "Shiver me timbers," and "Aye, matey," plus a "blimey" or two, a pirate can get by very nicely at sea. He doesn't even need to know the arcane names for the parts of a ship, since pirates typically point to whatever they're talking about, as evidenced by the proper way to sight a whale, namely, with arm extended and finger pointed while crying out, "Thar she blows."

In summary, piracy is an ideal job for a person who drops out of school.

Think before you decide.

Among the twenty-four who fit this description to a T are seven cousins from western Missouri, all of whom insist on being called Knucklehead. Fights frequently break out among the group, as one or the other claim to be the true Knucklehead, insisting that the other six are imposters.

Adding to this confusion are three crew members named John, known respectively as Big John, Little John, and John.

There is one Manuel, one Jesus, two Kim Lees (Kim Lee the elder, and Kim Lee the Fat, although in recent years Kim Lee the elder has become fatter than Kim Lee the Fat).

Rounding out the gang of reprobates are Queequeg, Jeff, Austin, Myron, Two-Feather, Patel, Curly, Larry, and Shawn.

Never in the long, dismaying history of the *Reprehensible* has there been a woman among its crew, and if this crowd has anything to say about it, never will there be.

But for the moment, at least, the crew is not in charge. The ship is still the captain's.

SETTING A TRAP

YOUNG CAPTAIN DEVILLE is so besotted with the vision of Jennifer Snow that while his ship lies anchored on the Atlantic horizon he dispatches his comparatively brilliant shipmate, Ruthless, the African gray parrot, to report on Jenny's comings and goings.

When Jennifer rides her Vespa to CVS Pharmacy to buy a box of Hollywood platinum blond hair color, Coop DeVille learns of her actions within the hour. When she stops after school for a slice of pepperoni pizza, or a burrito supreme, or a fried grouper sandwich, or a black bean and rice wrap in a jalapeno tortilla, Deville soon is in possession of these fundamentally useless facts.

But within a few days, Coop DeVille is able to predict when Jenny's Vespa will round the historic red lighthouse and buzz over the concrete causeway to Kansas-by-the-Sea Island in order to claim her preferred position for meditation and recorded music on Turtle Rock.

Thus informed, the young captain decides to set a trap.

On a warm, sunny Thursday afternoon, Jenny Snow pilots her Vespa straight from school to the Winn-Dixie on Military

Trail Road, where she purchases a cold bottle of cream soda and a package of Hostess cupcakes. She thinks about adopting the stray dog that's hanging around out front, but another girl beats her to it.

Oh, well, thinks Jenny, with a shrug. *I'm sure nothing will come of their relationship.*

With the refreshments stashed in the compartment underneath the Vespa's leatherette seat, Jenny takes a right on Indiantown Road, rounds the red lighthouse, zips over the drawbridge, and buzzes north to Turtle Rock.

Emerging from the dappled canopy of sea grapes into the bright South Florida sun, she pauses at the top of the weathered wooden steps and squints at a newly erected fence of wood stakes and yellow plastic tape that now surround the giant fractured boulder known as Turtle Rock.

The tape is imprinted with the words TURTLE NESTING AREA. DO NOT DISTURB. TURTLE NESTING AREA. DO NOT DISTURB. TURTLE NESTING AREA. DO NOT DISTURB. TURTLE NESTING AREA. DO NOT DISTURB.

And so on.

Nearby, brandishing a pickax, is a young man costumed in the outrageous attire of an Egyptian archaeologist from a previous century, or, more accurately, from the movies that celebrate that era—pith helmet, khaki breeches, and leather boots. The outfit is so out of place on this beach (or any other) that Jenny pinches herself to be sure she isn't dreaming.

"What's going on?" she asks.

"Oh, hello," Coop DeVille replies, extending his hand in formal greeting. "I'm Professor Dr. Hawkins-Smith. It seems we have a threatened species attempting to raise a family. Please keep your distance."

"A sea turtle laid eggs on the rock?" Jenny responds skeptically. "I thought they dig holes in the sand."

"Most do," DeVille agreed. "But once in a while you get one that's confused, and, of course, that's the one that needs the most protection."

Jenny remains unconvinced.

"What are you a professor of?" Jenny inquired.

"Why, turtlology, of course," DeVille says with confidence.

"Turtlology," Jenny repeats, her suspicion growing by the minute. "Don't you people carry some sort of official identification?"

"I left my wallet in my laboratory," DeVille says. "But if it's important to you, I suppose I could take you there."

"Oh, that's okay," Jenny replies, spreading a cotton towel on the sand and removing her cover-up to reveal a faded green bikini from two seasons past. "I'll take your word for it. How long will the rock be off-limits?"

"Until the eggs hatch," DeVille replies. "Which could take a long time—a year, possibly."

"Darn!" Jenny says. "And that's my favorite place, too."

Hoping to end the conversation with this peculiar boy, Jenny turns her back, opens the package of cupcakes, and gazes out to sea, where an ancient-looking three-masted ship, its sails furled and tied, lies at anchor on the horizon.

Brazenly, DeVille sits down beside her.

Jenny immediately jumps up, and without speaking jerks the beach towel from underneath the interloper and grabs her gear.

"No, wait," DeVille cries as Jenny slips into her cover-up and walks away. "I'll show you the eggs."

"That's okay, Professor Dr. Hawkins-Smith," Jenny replies as she hurries up the rough-hewn steps. "I wouldn't want to interfere with your important work."

"Argh!" says Coop DeVille as he hears the sound of Jenny putt-putt-puttering away. "That didn't work out at all!"

What a nutcase! Jenny thinks, weaving in and out of traffic in a manner that would have terrified her parents, had they known.

Without signaling, Jenny leans into a left on Military Trail Road, then makes another dangerous lurching left turn into the parking lot of the Palm Beach County Public Library.

Here, she hopes, she won't be bothered by crazy people in rented wardrobes claiming to be someone they're not.

For the next hour, she busies herself among the quiet group of studious souls at the library's computers, searching for whatever she can find about loggerhead turtle nesting seasons and antique three-masted sailing ships.

What she Googles up confirmed her darkest instincts: loggerhead turtle nesting season has not yet begun; the time from egg placement to the emergence of hatchlings is not a year but roughly two months; and the ship on the horizon is the infamous square-rigger of days gone by, the notorious *Reprehensible.*

Shiver me timbers, Jenny thinks. *Is that goofball a pirate?*

Although neither Jenny nor DeVille realizes it at the time, this is the moment when the tables turn and the hunted becomes the hunter.

A BIRD IN THE HAND

IF ONLY COOP DEVILLE had properly identified himself as the traveling bandito that he was, Jenny likely would have volunteered to sail with him, so great was her desire to escape her present unsatisfying life.

But because of DeVille's inept duplicity, a manifestation of the shyness around women so common among teenage boys, sixteen-year-old Jenny Snow plots to capture the gangly gang lord of the high seas and turn him over to the authorities, a project much more interesting than weaving potholders, or painting by number, or playing Boggle with her parents, or watching old movies on television until falling asleep.

And while her knowledge of the ways of the world is limited by her youth, Jenny Snow does not fail to observe that high overhead, as she whizzes home on her bright blue Vespa, a certain overly talkative red and gray parrot is following her

Perfect, she thinks. *The next move is mine!*

A return to the Winn-Dixie for a single item, then a short hop over to the Palm Beach Pup in downtown Kansas-by-the-Sea, and Jenny has everything required for the scheme that has popped into her head.

Once home, she opens her purchases.

The black wire dog crate requires no assembly, just the flip of a simple spring release. Opening the inner wrapper of the box of saltines is considerably more challenging. When her fingers fail to tear the waxy plastic, Jenny uses her teeth, scattering crackers all over her room.

No harm done, she observes. *Looks much the same as before.*

Jenny tosses the crackers into the crate, a training cage designed for housebreaking puppies, but to Jenny's way of thinking, a device with another useful capability.

Sometime during the night she is awakened by the sound of saltines being munched one after another. Without turning on the light or raising her head from her pillow, Jenny kicks the dog crate door shut with her right foot and, wiggling her big toe, switches the door to the locked position before falling back asleep.

"Uh-oh," a pitiful strained voice sighs from the shadows. "Should have seen that coming."

Early the next morning, Jenny stops by Turtle Rock, where she leaves a fresh gray feather Scotch-taped to the cover of a paperback cookbook: *Savannah Dinah's Favorite Fried Poultry.*

Okay, Mr. Pirate, Jenny says proudly to herself. *Your move.*

Until the draining of the Everglades got seriously under way, the sweaty southern tip of the United States was home to more wild birds than any other state, except possibly, and surprisingly, northern Alaska.

These days, while it's not unusual to spot a sandhill crane, a roseate spoonbill, or an anhinga drying its wings on the greens of a Florida golf course, you have to be a member of the club to do it, and while that's quite a lot of people—mostly old, rich men with colorful shirts and liver-spotted skin—it's nothing like it was in the old days.

Jennifer Snow, being as most sixteen-year-olds are acutely sensitive to the plight of Florida wildlife, including its panthers, sea turtles, alligators, pelicans, butterflies, bears, and bush hogs, takes special care to express kindness to her prisoner.

"Comfortable?" Jenny asks when she returns home, filling a stainless steel bowl with bottled spring water.

"Negative," Ruthless replies. "Want sunflower seeds."

"I'll see what I can do," Jenny promises.

"Dried apricots?" Ruthless adds. "Mustard greens, cashews, pizza crusts. Head itches. Scratch it?"

Jenny reaches through the bars of the dog crate and runs her fingers back and forth over the parrot's pecan-thin skull. It feels like a satin-covered eggshell.

"Ahhhh!" Ruthless says.

"Better?" she asks.

"Don't stop," Ruthless begs.

"Sorry," Jenny tells him. "I've got to dye my hair, tidy up my room, and be off to school. Why don't you just settle down and wait to be rescued by your boss?"

"Could be a while," the parrot admits.

"I have time," Jenny responds. "In fact, that's my biggest problem these days."

Before leaving, Jenny scrounges around in the refrigerator and comes up with a plateful of orange slices.

"How's this?" she inquires.

"Yum," Ruthless replies.

That evening the shower is running when Coop DeVille tiptoes into Jenny's room.

"Shhh!" he warns the parrot, putting his finger to his lips.

"Shut up, shut up, shut up!" Ruthless responds.

DeVille pauses to listen to the music coming from the bathroom. It is a thin, clear soprano voice, and it's performing an a cappella rendition of the vintage tune "This Magic Moment."

Deville finds it mesmerizing.

"Oh, my," he says.

Coop DeVille puts his hands to his chest, closes his eyes, and listens as Jenny's song casts a spell over his susceptible, seasick, lonely teenage heart.

But DeVille is first and foremost a pirate, he recalls, a seaborne thief, a scoundrel, and an outlaw, so with great determination he shakes himself free from the enchanting siren's song and begins to rifle through Jenny's room for something of value.

Discovering the gold locket, DeVille slips it into his pocket, liberates his parrot, and slips out as quietly as he has come in, just as Jenny is turning off the shower.

TALK OF MUTINY

ON BOARD THE *REPREHENSIBLE*, the crew is becoming restless. A collection of the world's roughest riffraff, these men have manners that are not improved by sitting still. They crave either to be robbing somebody or to be on the way to robbing somebody, if not pillaging an entire defenseless seaside town.

It is Knucklehead who first speaks the unspeakable.

"I think the captain's gone barmy," he tells the others at the table during a spirited hand of animal rummy. "I say we leave him on shore and get on about our business."

"Shhh!" warns another of the Knuckleheads. "If somebody hears you, you'll be scraping off the barnacles the hard way."

The Knucklehead is referring to a procedure known as keelhauling, a painful and typically fatal trip underwater in which the victim is pulled with ropes along the entire length of the ship's keel.

"Well, I didn't sign on to be a lady in waiting," the first Knucklehead says, throwing down a card, a full-grown kangaroo. "I'm a man of action."

Curly, who isn't playing cards but is sitting nearby in a deck chair with a hand loom, weaving a place mat for the captain's table, chimes in.

"I agree," he says. "We should be terrifying ships at sea and plundering settlements along the coast, not sitting here waiting for the captain to figure out his love life."

"It's a dangerous path this conversation has taken," warns Larry, thumb wrestling with another of the Knuckleheads. "But I can't say that I disagree with any of you."

"Well, I'm not doing anything until I finish this," Curly announces. "See how nicely it's coming together?"

He holds up the loom for the others to admire.

"I could use a scarf," says Kim Lee the Fat, who seems much thinner than when he first signed on. "It gets cold on deck sometimes."

"I'll make you one next," Curly replies. "What color do you like?"

"Hey, wait a minute," interrupts the other Kim Lee. "What about me? I need a scarf, too."

"You fellows line up and place your orders," Curly instructs. "I can only weave so fast."

With that, the first, tentative talk of mutiny on the *Reprehensible* subsides, but the thought, once planted, like kudzu vine on a county utility pole, grows ever larger.

That night, as the ship bobs up and down on the soft, rhythmic swells of the Atlantic, Captain Coop DeVille, feeling optimistic and generous, orders extra chicken wraps for the crew, which he directs be served with as many bottles of rum as his men can consume.

Meanwhile, Jenny Snow prepares scrambled eggs and whole wheat toast, a meal she intends to share with her feathery captive. Alas, to her alarm, she sees that the parrot has flown the coop. So too, she angrily discovers after a search of her room, has her antique gold locket.

So that's how he wants to play, she says to herself. *Okay, Mr. Pirate, you're on!*

The Turtle Rock Nature Preserve is closed to the public after dark, a legal nicety to which Jenny Snow has never in her brief lifetime paid any mind.

The post office is closed every holiday, she thinks to herself, justifying her actions, *but people still go there to mail letters.*

Such a way of thinking indicates that Jenny Snow has the makings of a lawyer—or a pirate.

Stuffed beneath the seat of her Vespa Jenny keeps a folded compact inflatable yellow kayak.

Once past the reef, she finds the sea to be only mildly moody and the infamous three-masted pirate ship a mere bathtub toy in the moonlight, an easy target for a young woman with superior rowing skills.

With the hopelessly drunken crew snoring loudly and scattered like seashells on the beach, boarding the ship undetected is a simple task. Jenny wastes no time locating the captain's cabin. A search for her locket turns up nothing, so Jenny hatches a different plan.

A pillowcase is all that's required to snatch and subdue the hapless Ruthless, now an avian shuttlecock in the ongoing badminton match between the determined Jenny and the overmatched Captain DeVille.

"Not again," the parrot mutters as Jenny lowers him to the kayak along with the Captain's navigational tools of compass, sextant, and tightly rolled maps of the charted world.

Still fuming over the purloined jewelry, she returns to the

captain's cabin to help herself to his cutlass, hanging conveniently on a peg.

Jenny is back in bed by midnight, and the hostage Ruthless, although briefly disturbed, is now enjoying cold scrambled eggs and crisp, dry toast in his home away from home: the dog crate.

"Stay put this time and maybe I won't have to kill you," Jenny advises the parrot. "Got it?"

"Awk," the parrot says.

"Jenny," her father calls from his bedroom. "Turn off your radio and go to sleep!"

"Okay, Daddy," Jenny replies. "Right away."

MAN OVERBOARD

UNDERSTANDABLY, Captain DeVille is furious.

His cutlass? His parrot? His compass?

Clearly, someone is out to humiliate him. Interestingly, however, DeVille's prime suspect is not Jenny Snow. Such midnight derring-do is beyond the capabilities of teenage girls, he reasons, so, naturally, his suspicions fall to his crew.

Given how they've begun huddling in small groups, then suddenly talking sports and other nonsense whenever DeVille passes within earshot, he concludes that the perpetrator of this irritating series of misdeeds is one or more of the illiterate Knuckleheads.

Given the total number of Knuckleheads on board, the odds are on DeVille's side, but if odds were all there were, the truth is that no one would ever win the Powerball drawing.

Yet someone undeserving always does.

DeVille instructs Henry to assemble the crew on deck.

"In a jiffy, Captain," Henry replies, although he continues to walk as slowly as always, the only speed his elderly body is capable of.

An hour later, he reports to DeVille, "I think I've found them all, give or take a couple."

"Thank you, Henry," DeVille says. "You're dismissed."

"Whatever is your pleasure," Henry replies, backing out of the captain's cabin as effortlessly as if he had been born with eyes on his posterior.

Most of the Knuckleheads plus Larry and one of the Kim Lees are standing on deck, shuffling their feet, clearing their throats, whistling softly, and generally trying to look innocent, an impossible task for any pirate, but especially so for this smarmy gang of scurvy miscreants.

"I'll give you men thirty seconds to return my cutlass and my parrot and whatever else you stole," Captain DeVille announces in his sternest voice, "after which, if I am not fully satisfied, one by one, each of you will walk the plank. I don't suppose I need to explain to you what that means."

"A board nailed to the deck?" offers one of the Knuckleheads, whose neighbor immediately punches him in his the ribs.

"Shhh!" he warns.

The other Knuckleheads and their comrades look at one another in confusion.

Cutlass? Parrot? they think. *You mean, this isn't about the mutiny conspiracy?*

"Now, see here, Captain," grumbles the biggest Knucklehead. "Methinks you're barking up the wrong mizzenmast."

"Argh!" agrees the Knucklehead standing beside him.

"Parrots fly," Kim Lee observes, reciting the accumulated wisdom of perhaps the world's oldest civilized culture. "Swords are very often left in adversaries or on the back seats of taxicabs."

Captain DeVille has no patience for imbeciles, especially

imbeciles who appear to be mistaking *him* for an imbecile.

"Silence!" the eighteen-year-old captain commands. "Return my belongings immediately or suffer the consequences!"

Then, under his breath, DeVille adds in a hoarse whisper to himself, "Worthless bunch of goons."

"What did you say?" demands the meanest of the Knuckleheads.

"I said you are a worthless bunch of goons," Captain DeVille repeats. "The stupidest louts and layabouts that ever sent their feeble brains to sea."

"I don't know about you fellows," Larry says, "but I'm not going to stand out here sweating in the hot South Florida sun to be falsely accused *and* insulted by some kid who doesn't know a spinnaker from spinach dip."

"Argh!" agree nearly all the Knuckleheads.

"I say we throw him overboard," yells one of them.

"Argh!" cheer the others, a cacophony that brings the rest of the motley crew tumbling on deck, except for the first mate, Henry, who remains in his cabin, polishing the captain's shoes until his own reflection greets him.

Henry sighs disconsolately when he hears the splash.

Although inconvenienced physically—indeed, he is in imminent danger of drowning—Captain DeVille has the intellectual satisfaction of knowing that he is right. The mutineers are stupid to a man.

Without his authentic pirate genes, with so many generations of evolved aptitude for the intricate ins and outs of successful thievery at sea, wherever those impulsive blowhards attempt to sail on the entire watery planet, they will be in over their heads.

Ha! DeVille thinks. *It serves them right!*

This thought occurs just before his own head is swamped by a wave, causing him to swallow about a quart of seawater and a small but surprisingly tasty jellyfish.

As fate has decreed, Captain Coop DeVille does not drown in the Atlantic Ocean off the coast of Kansas-by-the-Sea but is rescued by an early-arriving loggerhead turtle en route to Kansas-by-the-Sea Beach to deposit her eggs in the sand.

Deville grips the forward edge of the turtle's reddish-brown carapace—its upper shell—hitching a ride all the way to shore.

Stumbling onto land, he lies on his back while the turtle clambers up the beach to dig a hole, where over the next several hours she lays nearly sixty leatherlike eggs.

"Lord love a duck," says the exhausted DeVille.

A pirate without a ship is like a ship without a sail, a turtle without a shell, a teenage girl without access to commercial hair-coloring chemicals. While his mutinous crew founders aimlessly in the Sargasso Sea, having just discovered they have no maps, no sextant, and no compass, eighteen-year-old career pirate Coop DeVille wakes up in a landlubber's world, a fish out of water.

But even with family connections, you don't become a pirate captain without being resourceful.

Duct-taped to DeVille's flat stomach are two documents, one, the legal title to the three-masted square-rigger, the *Reprehensible,* the only piece of property that Coop DeVille owns free and clear (everything else having been acquired through criminal activity).

Even though it is not in his possession at the moment, on paper, the *Reprehensible* remains a valuable asset.

The future, if not assured, is at the very least subject to

mortgage. With his ship's ownership papers securely attached to his person, Coop DeVille is not worried about money. Any bank in South Florida would happily extend a handsome line of credit based on such a rare and valuable liquid asset, especially after the pummeling they received in speculative real estate.

But there is another important document affixed to the belly of the young pirate that is possibly of equal value to the title to his inherited three-masted sailing ship. It is the actual treasure map prepared by Tak-Ma, the Ugiri-Tom whose twin brother was being threatened at the time with a loaded blunderbuss held in the shaking, liver-spotted hand of one of Coop DeVille's dastardly ancestors, the notorious Salt-and-Pepper-Beard.

Unfortunately, Tak-Ma's map was created in haste, so it was not as precise as one might wish. But isn't that what they all say?

If only I'd had more time . . .

That's got to be one of mankind's top ten excuses, along with, "Nobody told *me*," and "I can only do one thing at a time," and "I'm sorry, I wasn't listening." Or the always useful, "I thought somebody else was taking care of that."

The Tak-Ma map has faded significantly over years of exposure to sunshine, seawater, and pirate sweat. Entire passages of instruction have disappeared, rendering it not so much a working map as a tantalizing set of general guidelines, sort of like the English-language instructions for assembling a twelve-speed bicycle or for a glass-fronted TV stand using only a three-inch Allen wrench.

But to an entrepreneurial young man like Coop DeVille, flawed though the map may be, it is entirely adequate for offering hope, for defining a direction, for providing purpose, for beginning life afresh.

Ah, the optimism of youth!

Onward! DeVille thinks. *Onward and upward!*

With very little folderol and a thick stack of papers, the Bank of America takes a ninety percent mortgage on the ship, while the venture capital firm of Dee, Tweedle & Thumper, a young, up-and-coming team of high rollers from New Jersey, who, having failed as a rock band have, with their parents' backing, gone into finance, happily advance a significant sum solely on the basis of the promises suggested by Coop DeVille's ancient, faded map, his captivating smile, and his charming piratical patter.

In very short order, Coop DeVille is living the life of Riley in an upper-floor furnished condominium facing the beach at Kansas-by-the-Sea, from which he watches the sunrise each morning and dreams of riches, revenge, and everlasting love.

THE OBJECT OF MY AFFECTION

WITHIN THE WEEK, Coop DeVille once again encounters our heroine.

The newly blond Jenny Snow is wearing a turquoise swimsuit, white flip-flops, and rose-tinted sunglasses, behind which she has donned contact lenses to change her eye color to sea mist green, an awaiting surprise.

To the recently dispossessed DeVille, she seems a goddess.

"Hello," he says.

"Where's your old boat?" Jenny asks, scanning the horizon and seeing nothing but a dive-bombing pelican.

"Ship, not boat," DeVille replies, "and I lost it to a bunch of dimwits."

"What does that say about your management skills?" she asks rhetorically.

"That I was outnumbered?" DeVille replies anyway.

"If that makes you feel better," Jenny responds.

Removing her sunglasses, Jenny now looks DeVille square in the eye.

Her sea mist green stare is like an arrow to his heart.

"Why are you following me?" she asks.

"I'm helpless to refrain," DeVille replies.

Jenny sighs.

"Persistence is a virtue up to a point, after which it becomes a nuisance, and beyond that a felony. It's called stalking," she advises him.

Coop DeVille hangs his head in embarrassment.

"I figured you'd disapprove," he says.

"Well, you got that right," Jenny retorts.

Now it's DeVille's turn to sigh.

The youthful buccaneer has lost his command, lost the ship that had been in his family for more generations than he could count, and lost the opportunity to impress the girl of his dreams.

Or has he?

Jenny has a choice to make. If she wishes, she can have Cooper arrested and slapped with a restraining order. Or she can take her chances and see where this thing leads.

Given her propensity for adventure, we should not be surprised that she chooses impulsively.

"Have you had lunch?" she asks, sealing her fate.

Although against the law, and unsafe, DeVille shares a seat with Jenny, clinging tightly to her from behind as she steers her bright blue Vespa through heavy traffic on Indiantown Road. Cruising up to the drive-thru at Wendy's, she orders each of them a cheeseburger, a medium lemonade, and large fries, then heads to her house, where she introduces her guest as Cooper, a classmate from Latin club at school.

"How nice," Jenny's mother says. *"Quo vadis?"*

"Thanks, but we just got some food," replies Cooper.

Jenny smiles.

The world has become her oyster, so to speak.

Jenny isn't sure how smart her parents are. Many are the

times she suspects "not very." But there is no denying that they are basically goodhearted people.

Jenny's dad shows Cooper his woodworking shop, where he's almost finished making a footstool. Jenny's mom bakes Cooper a caramel pecan pie to take home.

Clearly they are trying their best to be understanding parents, but it's not easy when your daughter is sixteen, pretty, headstrong, and ungrateful and her new boyfriend is an international felon.

Of course, Jenny's parents do not yet know this about Cooper, but deep down, as all parents do, they instinctively harbor suspicions.

Jenny's mother dismisses her anxiety by recalling the crush she had on the parentally unacceptable Elvis. Jenny's father considers his infatuation with Jane Fonda in the movie *Barbarella.*

Time heals all, they hope.

After her parents have removed themselves, Jenny sits in the living room with her captive young pirate. The two of them consume cheeseburgers and chatter like long-lost relatives for hours, during which he talks at length about the Ugiri-Tom.

Suddenly, without explanation, the youthful pirate sits up on the sofa in Jenny's parents' living room and begins to remove his shirt.

Jenny gasps.

Her sea mist green eyes become as big the eyes of those children that you see in framed pictures painted on black velvet for sale in abandoned gas stations and parking lots.

You know—unusually big.

Startled.

"Now hold on, Romeo," Jenny warns, pushing DeVille away with a flattened hand. "Party's over."

"No, no," protests DeVille. "It's not what you think. I want to show you a treasure map."

DeVille carefully peels off the taped, folded, fragile reptile-skin document and lays it across the coffee table, where it completely covers Mrs. Snow's fan-shaped display of a whole year of *Palm Beach Illustrated*.

"The Ugiri-Tom statue is buried somewhere around here," he explains, pointing. "But the exact location is unclear."

"What's it worth?" Jenny asks.

"Millions," DeVille replies. "Maybe more."

"Who else knows about this?" Jenny continues.

"Just us," answers DeVille, his voice hushed and conspiratorial. "And possibly a couple of the Knuckleheads. Plus a drug-addled venture capital firm made up mostly of wannabe rock stars, and a handful of unstable island governments throughout the Caribbean, and their first world sponsors, mostly the major international corporations who have their hooks into everything—nobody of any consequence, really."

"Hmmm," Jenny says, intrigued. "So it's truly a secret."

"Pretty much," agrees DeVille.

Just when you hear one door close, she thinks to herself, *a window suddenly becomes unstuck.*

"If I help you find it, what's in it for me?" she asks.

"Twenty percent," DeVille volunteers. "That's twice what a Volvo salesman gets."

"I want fifty," Jenny counters.

"But I'm the one with the map!" DeVille objects.

"No," Jenny corrects him, surprising herself with her firm

negotiating skills. "You're the one with the problem."

DeVille fixes his eyes on his spunky adversary. Given his background, under any other circumstances, he would have prevailed, but Jenny, for whom adventure is no longer an idle wish but a clear calling, returns his stare with a look that could bend steel.

For the longest time, the only sound to be heard is the distant waves breaking against the rocks punctuated by the intermittent cry of high-flying, well-fed sea birds, plus some especially loud snoring from the Snows' nearby bedroom.

Finally, the young pirate blinks.

"Okay," he agrees. "But first you have to help me get my ship back."

Jenny doesn't hesitate.

Not unlike the day when Laurel met Hardy or Lennon met McCartney, with a simple, tentative handshake, one of the world's great partnerships is formed.

A MAN WITHOUT A PLAN

THE FOLLOWING DAY, we find our crime-inclined couple at Coop's condo by the beach, struggling to hatch a plan to get the *Reprehensible* back, but their ideas might as well be eggs from an infertile turtle.

Nothing is hatching.

"I know," DeVille announces. "We'll sign up for a Carnival cruise. Then, when the time is right, we'll over-power the crew and—"

"That's ridiculous," Jenny interrupts. "There'll be thou-sands of passengers on board. Not to mention all the chefs and nightclub acts. You wouldn't stand a chance."

"But they're mostly seasick old people," DeVille counters. "Plus a handful of amateur magicians and lousy comedians. Basically, it's the Poconos set sail. It'll be easy, trust me."

"Next," Jenny says firmly.

"A fishing charter?" DeVille offers.

"I don't think so," Jenny replies.

"Okay, how about this?" Deville announces proudly. "We commandeer a submarine."

"I have a better idea," Jenny says. "Why don't you just report your old boat as stolen and let the authorities take it from there?"

"I'm not on very good terms with the authorities," DeVille points out.

"Maybe," Jenny suggests, "you should learn to be."

There are those who say that true love only happens when opposites attract. Like the poles of a magnet, each affects the other until somehow, somewhere in the middle, a new, united, and stable point of view is born.

Jenny Snow is not, at heart, a criminal, just as her teenage collaborator hasn't been groomed to be a proper citizen, but as the attraction between them blossoms, reason begins to prevail.

"Then it's settled," Jenny concludes. "Now let me see that map."

Although the faded document that DeVille hands to Jenny has been soaked, bleached, sweated on, and folded and unfolded countless times, it remains a single, untorn sheet, thanks entirely to the Ugiri-Tom's primitive way of life.

Not having knowledge of the technology of papermaking, these innocent folk had recorded their most important thoughts on sun-dried iguana skin, using an indelible purple paste made from the root of the indigenous Kava-Lava bush.

With no alphabet, the Ugiri-Tom depended on an arcane arrangement of tiny pictorial shapes, sort of like ancient Egyptian hieroglyphs but considerably more complex.

For example, within the Ugiri-Tom language were many figures of speech, such as "Don't let the hut shadow strike your posterior on your way out," "Holy shark bait!," "You could have knocked me over with a spider," and "You bet your sweet do-danga," each of which was expressed in a sequence of no fewer than twenty-six peculiar and exquisitely rendered pictograms.

Jenny lets out a whistle.

"We'll never figure this one out by ourselves," she concludes. "We'd better take it to Uncle Daschell."

"Who?" asked DeVille.

"My mother's uncle, my great-uncle," Jenny explains. "He teaches cipher science at Florida Atlantic University. I'm sure you've heard of him. Daschell Potts? He's the one who cracked the DaVinci code."

"FAU? DaVinci code?" Deville responds, more puzzled than ever.

"Cooper," Jenny observes, "you've spent way too much time at sea."

Meanwhile, with no one firmly in charge, or a destination, a common cause, or even a compass, the crew of the *Reprehensible* has fallen to squabbling among themselves.

Factions form, fall apart, and realign themselves, only to be doomed by ignorance, jealousy, and suspicion. All camaraderie is lost.

Anarchy reigns.

Fierce Atlantic storms batter the venerable ship. Food and drink run low. The last of the video game replacement batteries is claimed by a crazed Two-Feather. An equally unstable Myron shoots an albatross right between the eyes. Not to be outdone, Manuel insists that he be addressed ever after as "Gilligan." Queequeg, the ship's carpenter, takes orders for coffins.

Inside his cabin, Henry hunkers down and works crossword puzzles.

"What's a six-letter word meaning 'miserable wretch'?" he asks himself aloud.

Without hesitation, and using India ink, he writes PIRATE.

UNCLE DASCHELL'S CABIN

THE HONORS COLLEGE of Florida Atlantic University is located directly across the brick-paved square from the Saint Louis Cardinals' spring training facility at Roger Dean Stadium in the lovely planned community of Kansas-by-the-Sea, created within our time by a handful of visionary Kansans who'd had it up to here with prairie winters.

Here, Jenny Snow's great-uncle Daschell Potts works on top-secret projects for the United States government while keeping up appearances by teaching occasional classes in code-breaking fundamentals to ambitious undergraduates.

A reclusive man, Daschell Potts rarely leaves his classroom/office/laboratory/residence—a cozy cypress cabin built by the government just for him on the edge of the vast Kansas-by-the-Sea Upland Wildlife Preserve: your tax dollars at work.

Daschell Potts's closest neighbors are alligators, gopher tortoises, and opossums. At night the alligators serenade him with a chorus not unlike the sound produced by male bullfrogs—although they would have to be very large male bullfrogs.

This pleases Daschell Potts because he knows that anyone who may try to sneak up on him from the back is likely to be eaten before arriving. A tall iron fence provides him with additional protection.

As Jenny and DeVille are parking the Vespa, Daschell Potts is sharpening his fading wits with a crossword puzzle.

"Hmmm," he says. "A six-letter word meaning 'miserable wretch.'"

Using a ballpoint pen, the elderly Daschell Potts carefully prints the letters to spell GEEZER.

Jenny pushes the intercom button and speaks into the primitive electronic box that Daschell Potts got from the Toucan Taco drive-thru restaurant on Indiantown Road after it was closed through the combined efforts of the KBS Department of Health and Food Safety and the South Florida Wildlife Protection Agency.

"It's me, Uncle Daschell," she says. "Jenny."

A buzzer tells her she is invited inside.

Picking up several days' accumulation of dirty socks, Daschell Potts kicks a near-empty whiskey bottle underneath the sofa and greets his grand-niece with an all-enveloping hug.

"I'm so happy to see you," he tells her, the scent of alcohol exuding through his every pore. "Please sit down and tell me why you're here—and who've you brought with you?"

"This is Cooper," Jenny explains. "He's my business partner."

"Okay," Daschell Potts replies with a wink. "If you say so."

After a few more pleasantries, including a light snack of chips and dip and several hands of blackjack—all of which Daschell Potts quickly wins—Jenny unfolds the map.

"Holy shark bait!" the aging code breaker exclaims. "It's Ugiri-Tom!"

"You know about the Ugiri-Tom?" asks DeVille.

"Uncle Daschell knows something about everything, Cooper," Jenny says, patting her impatient partner's knee. "Give him a chance to explain."

"I'm not sure nature has allotted him that much time," mutters DeVille, who's detected the inebriated condition of his host.

Daschell Potts adjusts his eyeglasses and holds the map inches from his bulbous red nose. He turns the ancient document sideways, then upside down, then right-side up again, after which he places it on the coffee table, takes a sip from his icy drink—a honey-colored beverage in a mayonnaise jar—and closes his eyes.

From the pine and palmetto woods out back comes the deep-throated call of a very large reptile followed by the desperate squeal of a much smaller animal.

"Uncle Daschell?" Jenny asks. "Are you okay?"

The old man looks at his grand-niece and smiles benevolently.

"When I first set eyes on this," he says, "you could have knocked me over with a spider. I'm ninety-nine percent certain it's the language of the Ugiri-Tom, a now vanished island people, but it's a dialect I'm not familiar with. Of course, the Ugiri-Tom weren't well educated. Often they simply made up words as they went along, much as our present society does with facts."

"Do you think you can translate it?" Jenny asks.

"To be honest, I don't know," Jenny's great-uncle replies. "Some of it, sure. But then you come across a sequence like this"—he points to six tiny turtles in a row followed by four identical purple coconuts—"you have to wonder if maybe the guy who created this not only was uneducated, but had a severe stammer—not that that's anything to be ashamed of."

"Perhaps he'd simply been drinking," DeVille suggests sarcastically.

"It's certainly a possibility," Daschell Potts replies, unfazed by his houseguest's hostile attitude. "The Ugiri-Tom were very fond of a beverage made from fermented manatee milk. Why don't you leave this with me for a few days and I'll see what I can do."

"Leave it with you?" DeVille responds with alarm.

"Just for a few days," the old code breaker replies.

"For a few days?" DeVille repeats, clearly concerned.

In the manner in which one might greet a neighbor's new baby, Daschell Potts leans forward, smiles broadly, and speaks slowly and distinctly to DeVille.

"I wonder," Potts enunciates, "have you ever considered consulting a hearing specialist?"

THAR SHE BLOWS!

JENNY AND DEVILLE are seated in the sparsely filled stands of Roger Dean Stadium, eating Sno-Kones and watching the Kansas-by-the-Sea Hay Bales give up a promising three-run lead to the Jupiter Hammerheads.

"Are you sure it's safe?" DeVille asks.

"I think that guy got thrown out," Jenny replies. "But with that umpire, it's hard to know for sure."

"No, not the play," DeVille clarifies. "I'm talking about the map."

"Uncle Daschell isn't going to steal the map," Jenny says firmly. "I've known him all my life."

"And I've had that map all my life!" DeVille retorts. "Anyway, I'm more worried about him losing it than stealing it. He seems irresponsible. All beverage. No ballast."

"We all have our faults," Jenny observes. "But to set your mind at ease, he can't possibly lose it, because he never leaves his house."

With a solid thwack, a pop fly soars high above the outfield, where for a fleeting moment it disappears into the bright South Florida sun, but instead of falling back to earth to be caught by the Hammerheads' multicultural left fielder Juan Tu, it appears to circle overhead before fluttering to the second-level seats, where it lands right in front of Jenny and DeVille.

"I find ship," it says.

"Ruthless," Jenny responds in surprise. "How'd you get out?"

"Please," the parrot answers, waving a wrinkled, vaguely reptilian claw dismissively. "Don't insult."

"Hold on, Jenny," Coop admonishes. "Let him speak. He's located my ship."

"Where is it?" Jenny asks, her eyes still fixed on the ball game, where a triple play is in progress.

"Feed parrot first," Ruthless demands. "Then I spill beans."

"Why is it that everyone in South Florida seems to be working some sort of deal?" Coop DeVille asks rhetorically.

Fortified with a salty giant pretzel and a tub of slimy nachos from the Roger Dean Stadium snack bar, the African gray parrot is debriefed.

"Ten miles west of Bimini," the bird announces. "Half-day sail."

"Now you're talking!" DeVille exclaims. "Come on, Jennifer. Let's go!"

Jenny Snow shrugs.

Why not? she thinks. *Isn't this what I've been waiting for all my life? Or lately, anyway.*

An hour later, with Ruthless serving as airborne scout, Jenny and DeVille are setting out to sea in a chartered sixty-foot yacht named the *Mary Jessica*. That is, DeVille *claims* the *Mary Jessica* is chartered. It's hard to know with pirates.

The *Mary Jessica* is a well-stocked, fully equipped pleasure craft, most likely titled to some international corporation or entertainment industry executive. Jenny can hardly get over the luxuriousness of her surroundings.

"Man oh man, Cooper!" she gushes, nibbling on a chocolate-covered strawberry, which she chases with sparkling cider. "You've really outdone yourself this time."

"Glad you like it," the young captain replies matter-of-factly, as if there is nothing unusual about an eighteen-year-old orphan acquiring a multimillion-dollar seagoing vessel at the drop of a feather.

Closing her eyes against the sun, Jenny stretches out in the on-deck Jacuzzi.

"Hi diddledy-dee dee," she sings softly. "A pirate's life for me."

The rhythmic pulsing of the water in the hot tub, combined with the monotonous throbbing of the *Mary Jessica*'s massive inboard engines, lulls Jenny Snow into a dreamlike state.

In her mind's eye she pictures a wedding—*her* wedding—she is dressed in a flowing, pearl-encrusted ivory silk gown, attended by a dozen bridesmaids wearing iridescent peach-colored dresses. Pale, tiny orange blossoms flutter from the ceiling as a chamber orchestra plays Pachelbel's Canon in D.

It is the loveliest of daydreams, an idyllic interlude never to be repeated, and quite the opposite of what lies ahead for the impulsive, optimistic teenage girl.

Meanwhile, many miles away in West Palm Beach, in a practically windowless, cramped, nondescript two-story concrete-block building, Jenny's father, working beneath a painted sign that reads WE WON'T MAKE THE SAME MISTAKE TWICE! assumes that his daughter is safe on the streets of Kansas-by-the-Sea, riding around on her little blue Vespa.

Fathers know nothing about what their teenage daughters are up to, yet most daughters manage to survive their teen years and grow into responsible citizens anyway. This is sufficient proof that God exists.

Bimini offers even more proof.

It's the closest of the Bahama Islands to the mainland, a hop, skip, and a jump from Miami or Fort Lauderdale or Riviera Beach. It's got the clearest, bluest, most inviting water you ever set your eyes on. From on deck, you can see clown fish swimming three hundred feet below the surface.

Within this tropical paradise, the *Reprehensible* is foundering.

The ship has been reduced to a shambles, her sails tattered, her masts hacked with errant axes. Below deck, the sleeping quarters are littered with empty bottles, cigar butts, soggy magazines of an unpleasant variety, spent batteries, and crumpled frozen food boxes. The deck itself is piled with pizza crusts and rotting fish parts. Occasionally, without warning, a marble-size shot discharged from a blunderbuss whizzes through the air, fired at nothing in particular but deadly all the same.

Crossword puzzle in hand, Henry is at his wit's end.

A six-letter word meaning "without hope," Henry reads.

Looking up from the page, he glances out the porthole to see the *Mary Jessica* bearing down on the *Reprehensible.*

DOOMED, he writes hastily before locking himself in the captain's bathroom.

Daydreaming of a romantic wedding, Jenny Snow is startled from her reverie.

"Battle stations!" DeVille calls out, expertly swinging the "borrowed" *Mary Jessica* broadside.

"What am I supposed to do?" Jenny hollers back.

"Here!" cries Deville.

He tosses Jenny an antique double-barreled firearm. She catches it on the second bounce.

"Now what?" she asks.

"Shoot at anything that doesn't surrender," DeVille instructs.

I can't do that, Jenny thinks to herself. *I might hurt somebody.*

Aboard the *Reprehensible,* Curly, Larry, and Shawn are busy uncovering the cannons, a process made more difficult by the countless slippery slices of pepperoni pizza and fish guts underfoot.

Shawn, a naturally clumsy man, skids across the deck, striking a hastily convened conference committee consisting of Kim Lee (the fat), Little John, Jesus, and two of the Knuckleheads, sending them flying like bowling pins before hitting his head against the brass railing and passing out cold.

Attempting to regain his footing, one of the scattered Knuckleheads tumbles into the overweight Patel, who in turn falls against Jeff and John, knocking both of them overboard.

The battle has begun.

Between the two ships, smoke rises as bullets whiz through the air like bumblebees in a summer meadow.

A cannonball arches over the *Mary Jessica* and splashes into the water, where it strikes a good-size grouper much too curious for its own good. Myron dives into the water to retrieve it for dinner.

"When properly prepared, there's nothing that tastes better," he affirms.

Standing his ground, so to speak, Two-Feather launches a

flaming arrow at the attacking ship, and it lands near Jenny's feet. Intuitively, she douses the fire with the remnants of her cider.

Angry now, and rising to the urgency of the situation, Jenny fires her weapon into the air. The pistol ball strikes a passing pelican (truly unfortunate), which spirals lifelessly, beak down, into Two-Feather's foot.

"Ow!" he cries, hopping helplessly in circles.

The Kunckleheads, having no other weapons, immediately at hand, begin flinging batteries, which bounce like Ping-Pong balls across the *Mary Jessica*'s polished deck.

Lighting a fuse with his Bic lighter, an irate Jeff fires a cannonball at the *Mary Jessica,* where it tears a hole in the side of the hot tub, sending steaming water over the starboard side into the warm Caribbean.

"Okay, now you've really made me mad," Jenny declares.

As the *Reprehensible* tacks to secure a better cannon position, Jenny fires her second shot into the pirate ship's stern, where it splinters the tiller, disabling the ancient square-rigger's steering, while DeVille, armed to the teeth, blasts relentlessly at the quarterdeck, scattering the hapless, discouraged crew, some of whom retreat to the hold, as the others dive for the relative safety of the calm Bahamian sea.

Within twenty minutes it is all over. Kim Lee (the elder, though by now conspicuously fat) raises the white flag. Assigning the bikini-clad Jenny to the helm of the *Mary Jessica,* Captain Coop DeVille boards the *Reprehensible* and accepts the swords, knives, cutlasses, numchucks, and firearms of the half-dozen embarrassed crew members who dare to show their faces. The others are quickly rounded up and locked in the brig.

"All right, then," DeVille announces. "Now let's get a few things straight, shall we?"

Fights are intense, but someone eventually wins. That's when the real figuring out takes place. It's a dilemma known as "Now what?"

That night, over a dinner of fresh-baked pelican and batter-fried grouper, DeVille, Henry, and Jenny weigh their options.

"Please pass the gravy," says DeVille, deep in thought.

THE MANY LIVES OF DASCHELL POTTS

SO LONG AS we're on the subject of food, it's worth mentioning that Daschell Potts is no spring chicken. The old man has out-lived most of his enemies and enjoyed the equivalent of no fewer than three full lives: a prize-winning children's novelist; a prosperous ferret rancher; and, most recently, an expert on ciphers and dead languages.

Somewhere within this long, convoluted history is the rumor that Daschell Potts was killed by a runaway electric scooter; tried his hand at being an environmental terrorist; and, for the briefest time, worked as a school bus driver, but none of this has been proved.

All that is known about him now is that he prefers to keep his own company and is a crackerjack at figuring out words and phrases that others hope to keep secret.

The map that Jenny and her nervous colleague left behind tantalizes Daschell Potts. Faded though it is, the shape of the hand-drawn shoreline is unmistakable. It is somewhere on the Atlantic coast of South Florida—but where?

The clues are drawn in a sort of pidgin rune, a faux lan-guage for which the only precedent Daschell Potts knows is the crude alphabet of the Ugiri-Tom. But the problem with written Ugiri-Tom speech is that no two natives expressed it in exactly the same way. It is a fluid, free-flowing tongue, one without rules or structure, the linguistic equivalent of American jazz.

With Ugiri-Tom, Daschell Potts realizes, anything goes. Even strings of turtles and coconuts all in a row.

The old code breaker looks at the plastic teapot-shaped kitchen clock. It's nine a.m. He pours himself half a jarful of blended whiskey, filling the rest of the container with ice. This is going to be a tough one, he knows. Best to be prepared.

But before he can wet his lips, there comes a knock at the door. Daschell Potts quickly consumes the contents of the jar — waste not, want not — and shoves the Ugiri-Tom treasure map behind the refrigerator.

Who knows what trouble may be lurking outside? he reasons.

But it's only Lonnie, the FedEx man, delivering a big corrugated carton containing a full set of stainless steel cookware from the Cooking Club of America, that, to be honest, Daschell Potts has completely forgotten ordering.

Oh, well, he thinks. *I'm sure it will come in handy.*

Immediately, the old man begins to unpack the present from himself.

Half an hour later, with the pots, pans, roasters, lids, and stainless steel forks and spatulas rinsing in Daschell Potts's automatic dishwasher (What a great invention!) he prepares to return to what he was doing before he was interrupted.

But what was it?

For the life of him, Daschell Potts cannot remember.

Making breakfast?

No, the still wet beverage jar on the countertop suggests otherwise.

Doing laundry?

The dirty socks scattered across the floor suggest not.

Possibly he was planning to walk the dog, but no, he suddenly recalls, he has no dog, although, come to think of it, he's always wanted one. Perhaps he'll stroll down to the Palm Beach Pup and get one after he's finished with . . . with . . .

What?

Danged old fool! he chastises himself. *I hate it when this happens!*

He picks up a crossword puzzle to try to sort things out. A three-letter word meaning "forgetful," it asks.

OLD, writes Daschell Potts.

Outside, oblivious to the bull alligator serenade rising from the piney woods, a pair of gopher tortoises amble across Daschell Potts's lawn, where they pause occasionally to sample the low-growing vegetation in Daschell Potts's sandy soil.

The large, lumbering, endangered reptiles are observed with amusement by a small flock of sandhill cranes, tall, stalky, clever birds who prefer the scruffy lawn of Potts's house to the chemically treated fairways of the golf course. Nearby, poking around in the ditch in search of tiny backwards-swimming crustaceans, are three noisy white ibises.

It is a lovely afternoon in South Florida, Daschell Potts observes. *The perfect place and the perfect time to take a nap.*

BY THE SEA, BY THE SEA, BY THE BEAUTIFUL SEA

MEANWHILE, some seventy-five miles away in an equally picturesque setting, pirate matters are being settled.

At the softhearted Jenny's urging, the incorrigible castaway and imprisoned mutineers are provided with lifeboats, provisions, and a stern lecture from Captain Coop DeVille before being set free.

Unknown to Jenny, the motley crew will eventually arrive in Jamaica brimming with exaggerated stories about the intrepid "Bikini Pirate" and her daring exploits on the high seas. As the stories are embellished, she is awarded an ancient Ugiri-Tom name, *Vala-fem-del-Yugo,* which loosely translated means "the beautiful young pirate girl whose hair color is always changing."

Those who profess to be loyal to the captain, including the valet Henry and two of the Knuckleheads ("I don't know what came over me!" one says, while the other echoes, "That's goes double for me!") plus Queequeg, Myron, Larry ("The others made me do it," he swears), and Patel (obsequious to a fault, Patel presents the captain with a hand-embroidered banner that reads MISSION ACCOMPLISHED), remain on board to prepare the damaged *Reprehensible* to be towed just north of Palm Beach—the rarified playground of the superrich—to a rusting, rundown eyesore of a shipyard in Riviera Beach, a squalid, half-deserted hard-knock section of South Florida that looks remarkably like the near east side of Cleveland.

The laborers have to live *somewhere.*

Once his pirate ship is turned over to the fix-it men, DeVille wastes no time in divesting himself of the *Mary Jessica,* the subject of an official international law enforcement search ever since it first disappeared from its private slip on Miami's superexclusive Fisher Island.

Fisher Island is a place that is so fearful of crime spilling over from nearby Miami that it can be reached only by a seven-minute private ferry ride. Among many other modern luminaries, the daytime television celebrity Oprah Winfrey has a home here, as does the ex-wife of nighttime talk show royalty Larry King.

Although Jenny does not fully appreciate it, the ability of DeVille to obtain a yacht from such a secure area reveals volumes about his superior piracy skills.

"I'm going to miss that boat," Jenny says.

"It was just a rental," DeVille replies modestly. "There are lots more where that came from."

BACK TO BUSINESS

IT TAKES A LOT OF KNOCKING and button pushing to get Great Uncle Daschell to answer the door.

"Keep your shirt on," he calls amid a lot of clattering and glasslike clanks.

The door opens just a crack.

"What?" he says.

"It's Jenny," she announces. "I'm here with Cooper, remember? You've been working on our map."

"Who?" Daschell Potts inquires.

"Jenny, your grand-niece," Jenny repeats. "We've come about the treasure map."

"Are you lost?" Daschell Potts asks, opening the door wide to admit his young relative and her friend.

"Our map," Jenny clarifies. "You were going to decipher it for us, Uncle Daschell. Don't you remember?"

"I was?" Daschell Potts responds.

"I told you this would happen," DeVille mutters.

"You shut up," Jenny admonishes.

"You said it was Ugiri-Tom," Cooper reminds the old man. "You do remember that, don't you?"

"May I offer you some spinach dip?" Daschell Potts asks. "I made it yesterday. Or possibly it was last week—I forget."

"Wise up, old bustard, and quick, quick, quick," demands Ruthless.

"Ruthless, be quiet," DeVille commands.

"Sit down, Uncle Daschell," Jenny instructs. "We have some things to catch up on."

After a touch-and-go exchange during which neither side seemed to be connecting, Daschell Potts suddenly sits up and says, "Six turtles and four coconuts! Of course, I remember. Who could forget that peculiar sequence?"

"You loony son of beach," Ruthless mutters.

"Ruthless, I'm warning you: pipe down," DeVille orders.

"Get the map, Uncle Daschell," Jenny suggests. "We'll go over it together."

"Hmmm," Daschell Potts replies.

"You do have it, don't you?" Jenny presses.

"Of course I do," Daschell Potts insists. "It's just that it's, uh, undergoing, uh, well, some extensive carbon dating at the moment. Why don't you kids come back in a few days?"

"Is that offer for spinach dip still valid?" DeVille inquires. "And maybe a ginger ale?"

"No sweat," Mr. Potts responds. "Back in a flash."

"Like to see that, oh, yeah," Ruthless says.

"Ruthless, that mouth of yours is going to get you into nothing but trouble," Jenny warns.

Later, outside, from the back of the Vespa, DeVille shouts into Jenny's ear, "I know I already said I told you so, but I told you so, and now we have a problem."

"He'll find it," Jenny calls back. "He's just forgotten where he put it."

"What a fine kettle of fish this is," Coop DeVille observes.

"Cooper," Jenny observes, "people are people. You can't make them into what you want them to be. They're just who they are. Okay?"

"Argh!" replies DeVille.

Few eighteen-year-old pirates living their lives primarily at sea have mastered many social skills. Fewer still have learned patience for the foibles of others.

Meanwhile, Jenny's father is in his West Palm Beach office correcting a story that appeared in his magazine the week before about a newlywed teen queen. According to recently received information, the popular young celebrity had not shot at her husband but had merely shouted at him.

Darren Snow, the beleaguered managing editor of *Corrections* magazine, sighs, something he does quite a lot of. He finds his work is increasingly unsatisfying, his artistic wife more distant, and his daughter, a vague yet hotheaded teenager, a complete mystery.

What is she doing with her time?

What is she doing with her life?

What will become of her now?

Again, he sighs.

Although goodness knows he's tried, Darren Snow does not approve of Jenny's boyfriend, a sullen fellow who seems much too old (and worldly-wise) for his impressionable and pretty daughter.

"Snow!" carps the publisher over the intercom in the telephone at Darren Snow's elbow. "You got the name of the president wrong. It's Bush, with a 'B,' not Flush with a 'FL.' Please prepare a correction right away."

"That's why I'm here, sir," Darren Snow replies, quietly seething.

Someday, he thinks to himself, *I'm going to quit this job and sail around the world.*

In this respect, Darren Snow has more in common with his only child than he realizes. Each has been born with the genetic sequence for wanderlust.

Before leaving that afternoon, Darren Snow corrects a report about a missing yacht from the ritzy Fisher Island.

"The sixty-foot *Mary Jessica* mysteriously reappeared in its slip one week after being reported missing by its owner, the thirty-something heir to the Bacardi rum fortune," Darren Snow writes. "According to an eyewitness, Mrs. Aaron Feldman, wife of the best-selling diet author and famed Botox pioneer, the ship appears to have been struck repeatedly by seventeenth-century cannonballs.

"The craft's owner dismissed Mrs. Feldman's account as 'the hysterical hallucinations common to women who dote on small, yappy dogs.'

"As is our custom, a correction will be forthcoming next week."

And for many weeks to come, I'm sure, thinks the discouraged journalist.

At dinner that night, Darren Snow attempts to engage his only child in conversation about her day.

"So," he asks, "seen any good movies lately?"

"Excuse me," Jenny replies, pushing her chair away from the table, "but it's been a long day and I'm not all that hungry."

With the *Reprehensible* in drydock and the Ugiri-Tom

iguana-skin map misplaced behind Daschell Potts's refrigerator, the treasure hunt of the ocean's answer to Romeo and Juliet has come to a standstill.

To pass the time, Jenny and Coop ride the Vespa every afternoon to Turtle Rock.

By now, there are a number of squares of sand partitioned off by genuine turtle nest warnings. Beneath the coarse gray Atlantic sand, leathery loggerhead eggs slow-bake themselves to maturity.

While Jenny and her pirate pal listen to music on twin iPods, Ruthless amuses himself by harassing hermit crabs, one of which he eats.

"Patooie!" the parrot spits after swallowing a wriggling crustacean whole. "Nasty little vacuole."

STICKY FEATHERS

As AN ELEMENTARY SCHOOL art teacher, Jenny Snow's mother is especially dependent upon her hot glue gun. This rudimentary but reliable hand-held appliance has gotten her through many a complex classroom project (featuring nuts, leaves, buttons, dried pasta, dryer lint, and newspaper scraps), many an emergency (some artistic, some involving youthful wardrobe failures), and many a school-wide Parents Night exhibition at the Saint Hibiscus Elementary School in Kansas-by-the-Sea.

In fact, so important is her glue gun to Mrs. Snow's career (and sense of well-being) that she has by now collected not one but eleven of the electrical devices, in various sizes and amperage, as a post-impressionist artist might once have collected fine horsehair, sable, and ferret-whisker brushes.

Mrs. Snow also keeps a minimum of half a dozen cases of cylindrical glue sticks in the back of the crisper drawer in her side-by-side Kelvinator refrigerator, just to be on the safe side.

What if she should run out?

To Vanessa Snow's point of view, there is little on this earth that cannot be better appreciated by a vertical presentation on a public wall.

For one week, two years before, at the famed but seldom visited Edna Hibel Gallery in downtown Kansas-by-the-Sea, Vanessa Snow was honored with a one-woman show consisting entirely of junk mail envelopes arranged and glued into shapes resembling characters from *Winnie-the-Pooh,* the most creative of which, everyone agreed, was Eeyore in search of his tail: a credit card offer from the First National Bank of Medicine Lodge.

Many visitors to the gallery took photographs to share with distant friends and relatives, as a way of demonstrating how lucky they were to be living in such a wonderful place as Kansas-by-the-Sea.

For the distant friends and relatives, it was like receiving a postcard from Niagara Falls or the Grand Canyon or Roswell, New Mexico, printed with the words "Wish you were here."

A subtle but acceptable form of bragging.

Although Jenny's mother failed to sell a single art object, she looks upon that exhibition as her third-finest hour, her finest hours being subjects that are revealed later in this narrative.

Vanessa Snow is a restless woman, every bit as footloose as her daughter or her underemployed husband, although, sadly, none of them seems to recognize this trait in the others. She aspires to greater things, creations the likes of which no elementary school has ever seen before.

So when Ruthless begins hanging around the house with his endless and mindless and generally shocking vociferations, Mrs. Snow cannot help but take notice of his unique plumage.

With feathers like those, she says to herself, *I can make a wall hanging that will get people to sit up and take notice.*

Clueless, the African gray parrot chatters on.

"How is pirate like reservoir?" Ruthless asks.

"Beats me," Mrs. Snow replies disinterestedly.

"Both damned," Ruthless replies with an unnerving cackle.

"Mind your phraseology, birdy boy," Mrs. Snow admonishes her potential art project. "That mouth of yours will be your undoing."

That Vanessa Snow is an unfulfilled woman almost goes without saying. These days, most married people are unfulfilled, marriage having been revealed to be, like the practice of slavery before it, and the practice of routine employment in office building cubicles after it, a stultifying condition for the human psyche.

Only loneliness is worse.

As it turns out, the challenge that ultimately captures Vanessa Snow's imagination and holds out the promise of fulfillment is not the gluing up of gray parrot feathers into some sort of wall hanging, or the sudden transformation of her husband into someone daring, exciting, and dangerous, but a project precipitated by a rare mother-daughter picnic to Turtle Rock.

"Oh, my," Mrs. Snow announces on first viewing her daughter's semisecret hangout, a split seaside boulder as big as a Buick Roadmaster. "I can fix that."

"You can what?" Jenny asks.

"With enough glue," Mrs. Snow declares confidently, "I can repair that crack."

It's a good thing my mother has never seen the Liberty Bell, Jenny thinks.

Soon after the two consume a light luncheon of chicken salad croissants with mixed melon balls and stumble through an awkward talk about the dangers of spending too much time in the company of young sailors, Mrs. Snow mails an application for a grant to the Arts Council of Palm Beach County.

That through a stroke of genius she titles her ambitious project "Healing" makes all the difference. Within a month, Vanessa Snow has enough public funds for a truckload of glue-gun sticks, a big commercial-quality glue gun previously used only for the construction of high-rise condominiums, a two-hundred-foot orange extension cord, and a portable generator that can run forty-eight hours without refueling.

As for the effect of the noise and noxious fumes on the turtle nests and hatchlings, nobody seems to have inquired.

The process works something like the game of rock-paper-scissors in that development trumps art, art clobbers endangered species, and endangered species delay development, but only for a little while.

The clearances from the agencies in charge of preserving the coastline of Kansas-by-the-Sea take somewhat longer, this being vacation time for the federal and state governments, but eventually Jenny's mother receives them in the mail.

The result, however, is that Jenny Snow's meditation spot is now constantly occupied by her mother, and occasionally by a scruffy-looking photographer from the *Palm Beach Post,* a major life setback, in Jenny's opinion.

"Well, would you look at this?" Jenny's mother says to her daughter, shortly after planning the application of the glue.

"Look at what?" Jenny asks.

"Down here, deep inside the middle of the crack," she elucidates. "It looks like an old rusted cannonball."

Hmmm, thinks Jenny. *I should mention this to Great-Uncle Daschell.*

A CRACK IN THE WORLD

MEANWHILE, Uncle Daschell, having dropped a souvenir swizzle stick from the Reef Bar at The Breakers of Palm Beach underneath his refrigerator, comes across the misplaced map. To his credit, he not only remembers where he put Jenny's phone number, but he calls her right away.

"I think I've figured something out," Jenny's great-uncle announces. "Get over here as quickly as you can."

Jenny alerts Coop and breaks several of the more benign Kansas-by-the-Sea traffic regulations in responding to her great-uncle's urgent invitation.

"Look at this," Daschell Potts announces breathlessly, a physiological tic he's had ever since he passed the age of sixty. He points to a crease in the Ugiri-Tom treasure map.

"At first I thought it was a discoloration in the iguana skin," he confesses, "but if you examine it under a magnifying glass"—he hands his grand-niece a rectangular-shaped lens that he'd received free with the purchase of an unabridged dictionary from Book of the Month Club—"you'll see that it's actually painted on, indicating some sort of a rent or fissure in what is apparently a large object on the coastline."

"You mean it's a crack?" DeVille asks.

Daschell Potts sighs heavily.

"That's not only what I meant," he explains impatiently. "It's what I said."

"Turtle Rock," Jenny concludes.

"Exactly," Daschell Potts concurs. "And it's made all the more apparent by the symbols of six loggerheads and four coconuts. In Ugiri-Tom, the word for *coconut* and the word for *rock* are one and the same. Turtle turtle turtle turtle turtle turtle coconut coconut coconut coconut translates to Turtle Rock."

"Why didn't you mention this before?" DeVille inquires, clearly annoyed with Jenny's obviously daffy relative.

"If you must know," Daschell Potts replies, as peeved with Jenny's impertinent boyfriend as her boyfriend is with Daschell Potts, "I forgot. I've lived a long life and studied many subjects. Am I supposed to remember *everything?*"

DeVille shrugs. He has no patience for the elderly. To be honest, few people do, but it's a trait that's especially prevalent among eighteen-year-olds.

"So the treasure is buried beneath Turtle Rock," DeVille states.

Daschell Potts rolls his eyes. This no-patience position between the generations works both ways.

"So it would seem," Daschell Potts says.

"You're a genius, Uncle Daschell!" Jenny cries, giving her great-uncle a kiss on the cheek. "Thanks a million!"

"Think nothing of it," Potts replies, pouring three ounces of his *beverage du jour* into a Flintstones jam jar. "All in a day's work."

"Actually," DeVille corrects him, "it's been more like two months."

"Don't let the hut shadow strike your posterior . . ." Daschell Potts begins, but his voice trails off as he sips his drink.

"Well, then," DeVille speaks, "if you'll just return my property, I suppose we'll be on our way."

"I could do that," Potts answers. "But don't you think that under the circumstances it would be best if I made copies of the map? Not just for history's sake, but just in case?"

"In case of what?" DeVille demands.

"Pirates, for one," replies the old code breaker. "The government for another. Or am I confusing the two?"

"How long will that take?" demands DeVille.

"No more than a day or two," Potts says. "Scout's honor."

"Okay," DeVille says, reluctantly capitulating. "But you better not be pulling a fast one."

"Young man," Daschell Potts declares, pulling himself up to his full, pre-arthritic height of five feet and six inches, "if I were still capable of doing anything fast, I would not be standing here having this conversation with you."

Jenny giggles and tugs Cooper's arm. It's time to go.

THE BIG DIG

BENEATH A FULL, fat, pumpkin orange South Florida moon, Cooper and Jenny are digging in the sand. It is a frustrating exercise. No sooner do they scoop out an area underneath Turtle Rock than the ocean rushes in to fill it up again. Not to mention that despite the inspiring heavenly illumination, it is difficult for them to see what they are doing.

But alas, the teenage pirates turned treasure hunters are compelled to work at night because Jenny's mother's well-advertised fracture repair project keeps them away during the day, not to mention the severe legal prohibitions against disturbing a beach within a protected nature preserve in any manner whatsoever.

Loggerhead turtle nesting areas. Endangered species feeding stations. Pristine beach. Ecologically unique and fragile reef.

No digging allowed!

Lawlessness, however, is not a subject that deters Coop DeVille, and frankly, and most unfortunately for society, it's an attitude that's contagious.

Always one to run a red light or make an illegal U-turn, now Jenny Snow, like Bonnie in the persuasive company of Clyde, has begun to go along with her boyfriend's improvisational legal shortcuts.

On the third night, having made no substantial progress, Cooper leans on his shovel and expresses a thought that has been on his mind for some time.

"Has it occurred to you how perfectly convenient this is?" he asks.

"What do you mean?" his doting partner replies, still digging earnestly.

"That your great-uncle has deduced that the Ugiri-Tom treasure is buried underneath the very spot you choose to frequent every day," he explains. "I mean, what are the chances of that?"

"Chance has nothing to do with it," Jenny replies. "Uncle Daschell's analysis is based on facts. You saw the map."

"I've seen that map every day for eighteen years," DeVille says, "but it was never obvious to me that this is the right place."

"He's a trained professional," Jenny answers. "You're just a pirate."

Her words sting the young DeVille like the long trailing tentacles of a man-of-war jellyfish.

"*Just* a pirate?" he repeats. "Like, you think it's an easy job?"

"What I mean," Jenny explains, setting aside her shovel as the surf surges around her bare ankles and sand crabs scuttle up the beach, "is that Uncle Daschell has studied maps and arcane languages and encryptions all his life, so he knows what he's talking about, whereas you are merely guessing."

"Here's what I'm guessing," DeVille responds. "I'm guessing your uncle is an addle-headed has-been. Anything buried underneath this rock would be washed out to sea within a matter of weeks, if not days, and no Ugiri-Tom with a half a brain in his primitive peace-loving skull would dare to take a chance on such a thing happening to his tribe's most sacred treasure."

A loggerhead turtle, driven by instincts implanted three thousand years before, struggles past the two amateur treasure hunters to higher ground.

"See?" DeVille says. "That's what I mean. Even a turtle knows better than to dig at surfside."

"That's strictly instinct," counters Jenny.

"You prove my point," DeVille avows, standing astride the breech in the two halves of Turtle Rock like one of the seven wonders of the ancient world. "For the treasure to be buried here would be contrary to the laws of nature."

"Things change over time," Jenny observes. "Maybe the beach eroded since the treasure was put here. Maybe the sea is rising. Didn't the president recently announce his full support for global warming?"

"And maybe your uncle is pulling the wool over our eyes," DeVille replies.

"Just keep digging," Jenny orders, obviously annoyed. "You're much too suspicious of people."

But her partner's words stick in the back of her mind.

Six turtles and four coconuts, she thinks. *TURTLE ROCK. It is a fairly simplistic translation.*

Another week goes by, and all that Cooper and Jenny have to show for their efforts are enlarged biceps and sleep deprivation.

Jenny's mother, however, is somewhat successful. So far,

she's managed to pump about seventy gallons of costly plastic adhesive into the wide seaside fissure, and while this is only the tip of the iceberg, so to speak, it is an achievement, nonetheless—primarily of a financial nature.

Not everyone is approving of her activities, of course. Purists, unaware of the rock-locked cannonball, want to leave the rock as they believe nature made it. Or as nature made it *after* nature made it. Whichever.

A dentist, whose office is in a strip center across from a Blockbuster Video store and next door to a busy pilates studio on Indiantown Road, writes a letter to the *Palm Beach Post* suggesting that over time a procedure such as Mrs. Snow is undertaking will serve only to widen the cavity in Turtle Rock, not repair it.

"Basically, what this woman is doing is forming a giant wedge," he explains. "Ultimately it will cause the crack to expand. Had you asked me, I would have suggested a full crown."

Most people put the dentist's remarks down to an effort to drum up business for himself. Think of how much gold would be required! In Palm Beach County, with such nice weather year round and so many rich old people, there is fierce competition among medical professionals. It's not for nothing that South Florida is known as a jungle.

Meanwhile, Daschell Potts is having a problem. He has started out walking in the warm sunlight to the Kansas-by-the-Sea town center to buy a box of hand-rolled Honduran cigars, but halfway to the smoke shop he completely forgets where he is going and why.

Such sudden onsets of bewilderment are a common occurrence in South Florida, inhabited as it is by so many elderly individuals, who during daylight hours can be seen standing blank-faced at any given intersection. But knowing that he has company in his distress does not make Daschell Potts any less miserable. He hates these increasingly frequent bouts of mental confusion.

"Dang!" the old cryptologist says aloud. "This is *precisely* why I don't like to leave my house."

Looking up, he realizes that he is standing in front of the Kansas-by-the-Sea MultiCineplex 24 at which sixteen different films are playing on twenty-four different screens. At this time of day, the admission for senior citizens is only four dollars.

"One, please," Potts says to the ticket seller.

"Which movie?" she asks.

"You pick," Potts instructs. "It makes no difference to me."

Ironically, the motion picture the ticket seller chooses for Daschell Potts (and for some forty other old people who preceded Potts to the theater in a similarly puzzled state) is a documentary called *The Last Loggerhead,* a small independent French-made film that surprised a lot of critics when it was nominated for an Academy Award.

Although *The Last Loggerhead* failed to win the Oscar (losing to a romanticized recreation of the lives of Antarctic penguins, all of whom look exactly alike, so possibly the movie was made with a single penguin), the nomination was enough to assure *The Last Loggerhead* a couple of weeks of general distribution.

Even more of a coincidence is that the last loggerhead to which the title refers is not some living sea turtle clambering up a sandy beach to lay infertile eggs, as Potts presumes when he examines his ticket, but is a dramatized account of the perilous voyage of the Ugiri-Tom twins Tak-Me and Tak-Ma in their identical lashed-together outrigger canoes.

But Potts will not discover this until after a full fifteen minutes of coming attractions, most of which feature explosions, gunfire, and the futility of trying to reason with the walking dead.

CINEMA SIESTA

DASCHELL POTTS SITS in the cool, darkened theater, grateful to have survived the coming attractions and the animated commercial for the snack bar.

As soon as he takes a bite of popcorn, the movie begins.

As is so frequently the case with documentaries set at sea, much of the film is excruciatingly boring, consisting of lengthy episodes depicting non-English-speaking look-alikes paddling furiously in hot sun, high waves, and the occasional fierce Atlantic storm. And neither do the distracting French subtitles enrich the moviegoing experience.

Not surprisingly, then, somewhere during the largely fictitious adventure, Daschell Potts, like many of his seatmates, dozes off, missing the dramatic giant squid sequence completely, arguably the best part of the movie.

Potts awakens in time to see the landing, however, which the French film director imagines is something like the Pilgrims setting foot on Plymouth Rock, except that there are only two people involved, Tak-Me and Tak-Ma, and you can't tell one from the other, and they have to lug a seventeen-foot pearl statue to safety with a pirate ship breathing down their tattooed necks.

It takes a careful moviegoer to see the cannonball hitting and then splitting Turtle Rock. Everything happens so fast and there's too much smoke.

And another thing: strange things happen when words are translated from one language into another and then into yet a third language. Many common phrases get all bollixed up, sometimes amusingly so.

It's a phenomenon sort of like the game of telephone, in which children sit in a circle and one whispers into his neighbor's ear and the "secret message" is passed around until the last child to receive it, of course, gets it completely wrong, saying something like "The Watergate conspirators eat carrots," when in fact the sentence that began the game was "How much is that doggie in the window?"

The practice works similarly for Daschell Potts.

In *The Last Loggerhead,* the Ugiri-Tom expression "Don't let the hut shadow strike your posterior on the way out" becomes "Until we meet again" in French. Potts's retranslation of this phrase into English comes out as "Have a nice day."

What causes Daschell Potts to sit up and take notice, however, is how the French director has handled the Ugiri-Tom words for "Turtle Rock." Somehow, the great auteur has selected French words meaning "Marsupial Building Materials," but Potts decides that it is more clearly expressed in English as "Possum Wood."

Furthermore, the director of *The Last Loggerhead* has turned the Ugiri-Tom words "fractured boulder" into French words meaning "fish paste hand-ax waterway," which, to

Potts's trained, deciphering mind, can only be Anglicized as "Loxahatchee River."

As it happens, Daschell Potts's house backs up to a place called Possum Wood through which runs Florida's famous alligator-and-possum infested Loxahatchee River.

No wonder the peoples of the world have so much trouble getting along, Daschell Potts thinks, and not for the first time. *Nobody understands what anybody else is saying!*

The movie concludes with the Ugiri-Tom brothers preparing to bury their sacred seventeen-foot pearl turtle effigy in sandy soil as an opossum, hanging from a branch by its pink prehensile tail, looks on before being struck by the handle of Tak-Ma's makeshift shovel, a fatal act of clumsiness that causes the opossum to fall into the open jaws of a nine-foot, seven-hundred-pound bull alligator to a predictable conclusion.

The last word on the bottom of the screen is the same in English as in French: "Burp!"

When the theater lights come up, Daschell Potts admits to himself that the imagination of the French director is equal to his own vast education and experience. But together, in different places and at different times, the two brilliant men have inadvertently collaborated to solve the mystery of the treasure of the Ugiri-Tom.

The precious object is buried not on the beach underneath the busted boulder known as Turtle Rock, as Potts previously concluded, but is more or less in his own backyard!

In all his years, which are many, Daschell Potts cannot recall confronting such an astonishing coincidence. But perhaps that's not saying much, because recalling things is a subject that Potts struggles with daily.

Back on the sidewalk, the old man finds himself momentarily blinded by the bright subtropical sun. While standing at the curb to get his bearings, he suddenly remembers that he originally stepped out for cigars. Immediately, he sets off for the quaint little South Beach–style tobacco shop Castro's Chronic Cough.

Unfortunately, while paying for his purchase with his National Bank of Kansas-by-the-Sea debit card, he forgets everything he figured out while watching *The Last Loggerhead.*

Once again, the location of the treasure of the Ugiri-Tom is a secret.

THE PERFECT CRIME

JENNY'S MOTHER has at last completed her rock repair project. A photographer from *Palm Beach Illustrated* stands waist-deep in low tide to take her picture.

Vanessa Snow is dressed in a chic frock provided by the magazine for the occasion. Following the photographer's instructions, she poses awkwardly atop the boulder, holding two glue guns as if she is a high-fashion Annie Oakley taking aim at an unseen gunslinger.

Later, Mrs. Snow will buy dozens of copies of the magazine and send them to everyone she knows, all over the country, including people dropped from her Christmas card list years before.

Later still, she will look back upon this day as her second-finest hour, her finest hour, of course, being the birth of her daughter, Jennifer, and her third finest hour being the highly successful exhibition of decorative junk mail at the Edna Hibel Gallery in downtown Kansas-by-the-Sea.

Vanessa Snow eventually lives to be more than ninety-three years old, but in her mind she never had a true fourth-finest hour, although she certainly managed to perfect rosemary chicken casserole—everybody says so.

Alas, her moments of fame are fleeting, as they always are even for the most celebrated among us, including Goldie Hawn, Don and Phil, and President Andrew Johnson, to name but three, or, if you're a real stickler for detail, four.

Only one more professional achievement lies in Vanessa Snow's future, and that is when she is named Teacher of the Month by the principal of the Saint Hibiscus Elementary School, an honor based largely on Mrs. Snow's decision to have the children in her classes paint portraits of the principal of the elementary school for Parents Night. Smart politics, to be sure, but not what you'd call a true finest hour.

Actually, Vanessa Snow's finest hour is a scientific achievement of considerable magnitude, but no one will ever know the facts about it, not even herself.

It is not the birth of her mischievous, unruly child; or the flattering faux fashion spread in the society magazine of Palm Beach County; or either of her notable wall-mounted art exhibitions. No, it is the inspired pumping of three cement delivery trucks' worth of lightweight plastic polymer adhesive into what was previously a dense, heavy, and presumably immovable coral rock with a cannonball inside.

Once the glue dried, which, given its partial submersion in seawater, understandably took a while, it not only transformed what had once been two parts into one, but it altered the specific gravity of the entire structure.

This feat, combined with the effects of a month of tunneling into the rock's sandy foundation by a pair of teenage treasure hunters, produced consequences that were as dramatic as they were unique.

On a moonlit Thursday evening, with the tourists gone and

the tide coming in, determined to give it one last try, Jenny and Coop arrive with their shovels over their shoulders and a trash-talking parrot atop DeVille's head just in time to watch the great Turtle Rock float out to sea like a freshly minted iceberg.

"Holy guano factories in Hades!" curses Ruthless.

"Great Blackbeard's ghost!" adds DeVille. "I know your great-uncle Daschell is a loony, Jennifer, but now look what your mother's gone and done!"

"Don't you dare talk about my family like that!" Jenny snaps, slapping the teenage pirate's cheek so hard that the reverberations of the blow send Ruthless's tail feathers flying.

More affected by Jenny's outburst than by the startling sight of the partially submerged Turtle Rock bobbing off toward the horizon, DeVille mourns as the Vespa putt-putt-putts down the road.

"Maybe it runs in the family," he whines to his parrot. "Maybe they're all crazy."

"Argh," agrees Ruthless.

As luck so often has it, *Corrections* magazine is just about to go to press when Jenny returns home. On her way to fume in her room, Jenny passes her father in the hallway and mutters that Turtle Rock has just vanished.

Immediately, Mr. Snow telephones the scoop desk at his magazine, where an intern named Todd is playing a video game over the Internet. Spurred by his boss's excitement, Todd jumps into his Honda Civic to confirm the improbable story, then dashes back to the office to write the three paragraphs that will put *Corrections* magazine in the same league as the *Washington Post* or the *New York Times,* namely, the first medium, either printed or electronic, to report the brazen theft of the public Palm Beach County art object known as "Healing."

With nothing but a handful of sandy gray feathers to go on, and so many people in South Florida owning vast amounts of stolen artwork anyway, the police are baffled. They declare the purloining of Turtle Rock to be "the perfect crime."

RAMIFICATIONS

THE FOLLOWING WEEK *Corrections* magazine reports that only two feathers were found at the scene of the crime, not a handful.

As for Jenny, she never says another word about the incident. Not only does she want to forget what happened that night, but she is inclined to forget every minute she ever spent with that cocky pirate boy Captain Cooper DeVille.

Still, she cannot resist. She telephones him.

"Did you mean what you said about my mother?" she asks.

The pirate boy, accustomed to speaking his mind and receiving instant agreement, responds, "You have to admit that she's somewhat 'out there,'" he says.

"'Out there'?" Jenny repeats.

"Wacko," Cooper clarifies.

"I see," says Jenny. "And Great-Uncle Daschell?"

"Certifiably insane," Cooper declares.

"How do you feel about my father?" Jenny inquires.

"He's a doofus," says Cooper. "A blank slate that will forever remain blank."

"Well," says Jenny. "That just leaves me. How do you feel about me?"

"You're cute and you drive a cool scooter," Cooper replies eagerly. "Want to go out for burgers?"

Jenny hangs up the phone.

Imagine choosing someone like him for a boyfriend, she says to herself. *What was I thinking?*

BROKEN APART

JENNY SNOW AND COOPER DEVILLE are as separated as Turtle Rock was for so many centuries, half on land and half in the sea, and it's going take a lot more than Vanessa Snow and her glue guns to put these two back together.

How do these things happen so suddenly? wonders Jenny.

A few unguarded words and—CRACK!—it's all over.

The terrible power of words.

Together, Jenny and Coop are a pair of daring young adventurers hot on the trail of one of the world's great treasures, even though they don't know precisely what it is, but now, with each of them suddenly solo, instead of sailing the high seas, fighting pirates, digging for treasure, and cruising Indiantown Road as if the whole world belongs to them, they sit at home and brood.

Jenny Snow is in the semidarkness of her bedroom, holding a pencil and gazing blankly into the gloom. She is trying to think of as many words as she can form with the letters in the word *ennui,* an English word taken intact from the French, meaning "boredom."

She hasn't made much progress.

In. Nine. Nun. The problem, it seems, is an overabundance of vowels and a distinct shortage of consonants in what is basically a short word.

On the other hand, a name like DeVille, only slightly longer, and also borrowed without modification from the French, is rich with possibilities, *devil* being foremost among them, but also *live, led, ill, lie,* and *vile*—not a bore in the bunch.

"Jenny," her mother announces, opening the door just a crack, "unless you are quite ill, your father and I expect you to join us for dinner."

Jenny is annoyed by the interruption. She has just begun a promising deconstruction of her own name, Snow: *Won. Now. Sow. No. On. Wo!*

"I'll be out in a minute," she says.

Try as she might to escape her fate, Jenny's life keeps returning to boredom for as far as the eye can see.

Why, for all the action she's engaged in now, she may as well be a clerk in a museum gift shop.

Ironically, this is exactly what Burson, Jenny's younger would-be boyfriend, is doing these days—working as a clerk in the gift shop of the South Florida Loggerhead Turtle Rehabilitation Center.

Run primarily by volunteers and funded by small donations from ordinary people, the center consists of a scattering of cinder-block buildings, mobile homes, aboveground pools, and broad blue canvas canopies near the parking lot across the road from the beach. Even with cars going by all the time, you can hear the surf.

Burson works here Monday through Friday. The job doesn't pay much, but Burson is a boy who's genuinely concerned about endangered species. There are, of course, an abundance of these to choose from in South Florida, but Burson finds himself especially attracted to the plight of the loggerhead turtle.

Here is a graceful two-hundred-pound animal drifting with the Atlantic currents from Florida to Greece for as long as three years at a time before suddenly being summoned by some inexplicable, near magical force to the very strip of beach where it was born, where it does its clumsy best to beget another generation.

Burson finds this to be as mysterious as anything that nature has ever conceived, from quarks, to distant galaxies, to black holes in the fabric of the universe.

He also finds the loggerhead (*Caretta caretta*) to be astonishingly beautiful in its own special seagoing way, with its distinctive giraffe like-dappled head, its tapered, serrated carapace, long, angel-wing front legs, and small but surprisingly expressive eyes.

Dog eyes, Burson thinks.

Plus, the loggerhead turtle is such a gentle reptile, not at all like the ferocious alligators or darting tree lizards or lumbering, dust-covered gopher tortoises that keep the tourists all a-flutter.

It is not exaggerating to say that Burson has the heart of a Ugiri-Tom.

On his lunch breaks, Burson likes to visit the shaded tanks of the turtle yard.

Some of these displaced loggerheads were caught in

fishing nets. Some were injured by boat propellers. Others are sick from dining on plastic Wal-Mart bags or Pampers or other garbage discarded at sea.

The latest injured foundling is named Jenny—Burson's idea, of course—who's a young six-year-old in need of a full-time sponsor. Medical care, including medical care for sea turtles, is expensive.

Burson donates what he can.

Burson sits on a bench as the sun sparkles like stars through tiny holes in the canvas canopy. As he eats the lunch he's brought from home, he watches Jenny the loggerhead glide effortlessly around her blue plastic swimming pool. She lets him reach in to scratch her head and tickle her under the chin.

Someday Jenny will be gone, Burson knows, with no memory of her time with him. She is, after all, a medical patient, not somebody's pet. The marine life at the center is rehabilitated for a single purpose: to be released into the wild. After that, whatever happens is up to nature.

This is a thought that appeals to Burson: being released into the wild, living at the whim of nature.

Someday, Burson thinks, inadvertently expressing the motto of the founders of Kansas-by-the-Sea.

Someday.

"They told me that I'd find you here," a voice says sweetly.

So startled is he when he looks up to see the pretty, suntanned face of Jennifer Snow that he drops his bologna sandwich into the pool.

Meanwhile, DeVille, stuck in his condo without a girl, without a ship, without a crew, without a treasure to seek, and with only a foulmouthed parrot for companionship, finds himself quickly reduced to irrelevance.

Not to mention, he is lonely.

Before, Cooper had plenty of people around. Even if most of them smelled bad, acted worse, and were as dumb as bleached-out barnacles, at least they provided the young pirate with amusement and, on occasion, adventure.

And then there's the matter of the hole in his heart left by Jenny Snow.

Cooper sighs.

This living alone is for the birds, he thinks.

"Me hungry," squawks Ruthless. "Want pizza."

"Order it yourself," snaps DeVille.

He is in no mood for bird talk.

Cooper considers applying for a job, but the only kind that seems compatible with his unique qualifications is being the boss of a big international corporation, and he knows he'd go crazy if he had to sit in an office all day long.

To take his mind off his troubles, he tries reading, but it's clear he should have chosen more carefully. The book he took from the nearby branch of the Palm Beach County Public Library, *Ka-blam! The True Story of a Household Nuclear Explosion,* seems promising enough, but once he gets through the first few pages, in which a Winnipeg man accidentally blows up his neighborhood by simultaneously depressing all the keys on his microwave oven control panel while wiping it free of smudges with a foaming tub and tile cleanser, the story becomes as dry as dust.

(Ironically, originally written in Canadian English by a newspaper journalist named Luger Flog, the Palm Beach County Library's edition of *Ka-Blam! etc.* is a translation into

American English by a moonlighting Daschell Potts in his more lucid days.)

Unmindful that *Ka-Blam! etc.* is public property, DeVille tosses the book to the floor, then, in the last desperate act of the terminally lonely, clicks on the television.

The Kansas-by-the-Sea Hay Bales are sixteen runs behind the Mar-a-Lago Concierges.

Good grief! DeVille thinks, flopping backwards onto the unmade bed and staring at the ceiling.

Idly, he watches as a spider collects a mosquito that is futilely attempting to free itself from the center of a lacy web.

That's me, DeVille thinks. *Trapped and doomed to die alone in this dreadful place.*

A further examination of the ceiling reveals a series of minute cracks that extend throughout the plaster, not unlike the spider's deadly handiwork.

This in turn brings to mind the famous former cleft in the now oceangoing Turtle Rock, which, as what begins as random thoughts eventually connect in logical fashion like links in a golden chain, leads DeVille to consider the welfare of the Ugiri-Tom treasure map.

That he is continuing to entrust it to the care of Jenny Snow's unstable relative, the once eminent and now clearly demented man of arcane words, Daschell Potts, suddenly unnerves him.

I'd better get that back, DeVille thinks.

"Pizza guy need credit card number," squawks Ruthless, holding the telephone in his talons and rotating his head like an owl toward DeVille. "Also expiration date."

"How fast can he get it here?" asks DeVille, suddenly hungry too. "And did you ask for an extra large?"

MEANWHILES UPON MEANWHILES

EXCEPT FOR YOUR very last gasp of breath, everything that happens to you throughout your life is, technically speaking, "meanwhile."

So while Jenny is meanwhiling with her rediscovery of the softhearted Burson, and Cooper is meanwhiling with his long-time companion and champion cusser, Ruthless, Great-Uncle Daschell is meanwhiling—some might say "puttering"—around his house, unaware that he is being spied on from the building across the street by three overly curious men of advanced age.

Officially, the three Peeping Toms are Potts's university colleagues, although he has encountered them only once, where they blocked his access to the canape table at the Welcome Faculty brunch at the Chancellor's opulent home.

"He's definitely up to something," says Professor Dr. Dell-Finian.

"Yes, but what?" asks Professor Dr. Von Heron.

"That's the problem in a nutshell," explains Professor Dr. Lucius Birch, BA, MA, PhD, DD, JD, MD, and OBE.

Potts remains blissfully oblivious.

In fact, this is precisely why Coop DeVille has good reason to be concerned about the safety of the treasure map that he left in the liver-spotted hands of the notoriously absent-minded Daschell Potts. For just as the young pirate is pulling on a strand of warm mozzarella cheese in his rented oceanside condo, Jenny Snow's inebriated great-uncle is at home frying a skilletful of heavily breaded calamari, the first of several foolish steps in what is destined to be a treasure map calamity.

As it cooks, he steps outside to enjoy the new blooms of his patio garden.

Daschell Potts's patio garden is a perfect square, measuring sixteen feet by sixteen feet and hidden behind a brown privacy fence that is exactly eight feet tall.

That it is called a privacy fence is something of a misnomer, since while it is true that someone standing outside cannot see in, nor can someone standing inside see out, a multistory university building looms on the other side of the street like an arriving ocean liner. Anyone inside, including the three envious professors, can see everything that's going on within Potts's patio garden.

Oh, well, Daschell Potts rationalizes. *In a time when any fool can snoop through your library files, your medical records, your bank accounts, your arrest records, your divorce settlements, and every keystroke on your computer, there's no privacy left anyway. We might as well be naked and be done with it.*

Daschell Potts exaggerates to make a point. When he is in his patio garden, he is always dressed, although excessively casually, usually in flat-bottomed tennis shoes stained with bleach spots, no socks; a T-shirt with a picture or a saying, such as WAKE ME WHEN IT'S OVER or MAKE ME LAUGH; and khaki cotton shorts frayed at the hems from repeated washings in hot water.

On three sides of his patio is a two-foot expanse of dirt in which the builder planted hardy, low-maintenance, foreign-looking bushes at regular intervals. Potts has added a few items to the spaces in between, but mostly has concentrated on what is known as "container gardening."

Within his various containers Potts has planted lettuce, tomatoes, parsley, basil, chives, rosemary, oregano, carnations, bananas, dwarf oranges, limes, avocados, hibiscus, and six different varieties of flowering trees, none more than six inches tall, and none more than a couple of millimeters in diameter.

Daschell Potts's garden is truly a garden for the future.

It is, in short, an optimist's garden.

Each morning, Daschell Potts hoses off the patio and waters the plants. This being South Florida, something is always in bloom. The colorful carnations take center stage this week. Last week, delicate white flowers on the orange trees released their perfume before drifting to the patio to form a fairy bed. The halfdozen different herbs have found their way into Potts's food for days.

Daschell Potts sits on a teak bench in his patio garden. He closes his eyes. The sun and the scent and the light breeze are typical of South Florida. Having lived in many other parts of the world, Daschell Potts relishes these blissful days in this special place.

At this time of day, the loudest sound Potts hears is the cawing of a crow. It sounds like laughter.

Indeed, the lonely three-legged panther at the Kansas-by-the-Sea Volunteer Rescue Center has a bigger habitat, as do the three white pelicans with broken wings, the blind gopher tortoise, and the pair of flying squirrels suffering from acute anxiety.

Daschell Potts's patio garden is a place for sitting.

And sitting is the proper pose for thinking.

And thinking can lead to remembering all sorts of things.

On this day, as Daschell Potts squints to see a carnation begin to break through its flame-shaped case, he is surprised suddenly to recall the particulars of his Ugiri-Tom epiphany, namely that the Ugiri-Tom treasure has been buried all along in his own backyard.

Immediately, lest he forget once again, he starts to telephone his grand-niece with the news, but before he can complete the dialing of the seven simple digits, the acrid aroma of burning squid hits him like a thunderbolt.

"Oh, dear," Potts cries. "The calamari!"

Urgent situations call for urgent solutions. Potts lifts the smoldering pan from the stovetop and, searching in vain for the roll of paper towels he purchased the day before, settles for the nearest expanse of suitable material he can find: the map on the kitchen counter.

Centuries of seawater and sun have rendered the iguana-skin surface highly absorbent, and although it is not particularly clean, under the circumstances, it seems an acceptable paper towel substitute.

Improvisation being the hallmark of brilliance, Daschell Potts dumps the entire steaming contents of the skillet onto the Ugiri-Tom map.

PLOP!

The stinking, overcooked concoction immediately gives up two cupfuls of thick, brown, ash-laden grease.

It would be easy to blame Jenny's great-uncle for the near complete destruction of what was at least a valuable antique and at best a detailed guide to an artistic and material fortune.

But is this, in fact, the case?

Blame is so easy to assign.

Shouldn't DeVille have had the presence of mind to retrieve his map when he had the chance?

Shouldn't Jenny have been less in denial of her great-uncle's obviously failing faculties?

And why did the Ugiri-Tom rely on a material that would become so attractively absorbent after only a few hundred years of exposure to the elements? Does this represent the epitome of their product engineering skills, or were they too simply being expedient?

Surely, the millers and blenders and packagers and marketers of the boxed calamari breading kit (Uncle Bud's Five-Minute Calamari) have a hand in this as well.

Is profit their only motive for using gooey lard instead of a more refined cold-pressed extra virgin olive oil or a practically clear and more heart-friendly rapeseed oil, now known popularly as canola oil?

And what about the world's biggest retailer who sold the box to Potts? Does not its management bear some responsibility for what it stocks, or are they content to sell goods at the lowest possible price regardless of their quality or country of origin?

One could cite the builder of Potts's home for not installing a simple plastic paper towel rack. How much would that have cost?

Cheapskates.

It is possible to find fault with the entire popular culture for collectively insisting that paper towels be deemed a necessary part of our lives.

What did people do before this modern disposable landfill-threatening convenience was invented? Use cloth towels? Eat more grease? How did his grammy in Memphis make fried chicken taste so good all those years?

Heck, a case could even be made against Burson and people like him, for isn't Burson a self-professed squid lover? Or is that turtles?

The list of those responsible for the Ugiri-Tom treasure map disaster could easily continue for pages, for, like the spider's web, or golden chains of thought, all action is interconnected.

There is no escaping this fundamental fact.

A man in Potts's physical condition shouldn't be eating fried foods in the first place. Doesn't he know that? Who is responsible for informing him?

It's his doctor's fault. It's his parents' fault. It's the media's fault. It's the government's fault.

When Coop DeVille, arriving at Potts's doorstep, discovers what has happened to the precious object he personally protected for his entire life, he breaks down and cries like a little baby.

Feeling sorry for the troubled teen, and assuming that his expression of grief has to do with a misunderstanding between DeVille and Jenny, Daschell Potts offers to share his blackened but still warm calamari with the boy and his potty-mouthed parrot.

"Thanks anyway," DeVille says, sniffling. "We just ate."

From every disaster arises some good. The accidental obliteration of the ancient Ugiri-Tom diagram fixes the location of the Ugiri-Tom treasure in Daschell Potts's head forever. He now knows it better than he knows the back of his hand, the spots of which seemed to change daily.

At the same time, Jenny's chance discovery of a dusty paperback book at the gift shop of the South Florida

Loggerhead Turtle Rehabilitation Center called *The Winged Goddess of the Sea,* enables her to identify the object of her pirate quest as a seventeen-foot effigy of a loggerhead turtle constructed entirely of mother-of-pearl.

Holy caretta! Jenny thinks. *I'd better go see Uncle Daschell.*

DEFACE IN THE CROWD

"I DIDN'T EXPECT to find you here," Jenny says.

"I came for my map," explains DeVille, still sniffling from the news Daschell Potts has given him.

It's an awkward moment for everyone in the room.

Finally, DeVille pulls himself together and, exhibiting the natural leadership ability that comes from being a pirate captain, extends a hand of greeting to Burson.

"DeVille," he says firmly.

"Burson," Burson replies.

"Potts," adds Great-Uncle Daschell, thinking it must be his turn.

"Snow," says Jenny, hoping to conclude the embarrassing and in her mind entirely unnecessary ritual foisted upon a naive world by men countless years ago.

But it is Ruthless who demands the last word.

"Possum poop," the African gray mutters.

"Is that your name or your cologne?" inquires Burson in a rare and unfortunately unsuccessful attempt at humor.

"Well," announces Daschell Potts, "now that we all know each other, let's get down to business, shall we?"

He steps into his kitchen and returns with the dripping, blackened iguana skin that once depicted the location of the priceless treasure of the Ugiri-Tom.

Like some do when watching a horror movie in a darkened theater, DeVille averts his gaze, waiting for the moment to pass.

"It looks a lot different, Uncle Daschell," Jenny points out. "Did you use a special treatment on it?"

"You could say that," her aging relative replies.

The tension in the room is great. So intense, in fact, that you can cut it with a letter opener, if you have one, as one of the visitors, in fact, does.

The situation has reached that point when, in a traditional drawing room mystery, the suspects gather together for the announcement of whodunnit: Jenny, Burson, DeVille, Great-Uncle Daschell, Ruthless, and the unseen presence of three sets of professorial eyes staring from the university building across the street.

Except in this case, Uncle Daschell does not announce whodunnit.

He reveals what and where it is.

"About the treasure," he begins. "Initially, all those turtles and coconuts confused me. But since the map is written in a language that has absolutely no standards, the information contained therein is actually in a code within a code within a code. Unfortunately, I approached it the way your father, Jenny, might try to understand hip-hop music. Understandably, a huge waste of time."

"Yeah," Jenny agrees with a laugh. "He'd be publishing corrections until the end of time."

"All those weeks of useless digging," DeVille moans,

turning to Jenny. "Didn't I try to tell you?"

"You seemed to be having a good enough time on the nights we were alone," Jenny snaps at DeVille.

She sidles over to be closer to Burson, who, instinctively, places his right arm around her waist, a motion that takes Jenny by surprise. Neither is the possessive gesture lost on a glowering DeVille.

"Well, don't ask me anything," Burson chimes in cheerfully. "I just came along for the ride on Jenny's Vespa. My interest is in loggerhead turtles, not buried treasure."

"I can tell you with absolute certainty that you'll find both right back there," Great-Uncle Daschell says.

He gestures over his shoulder with a fat, crooked thumb. Jenny notices that it has an unsightly hangnail.

"In the kitchen?" DeVille responds.

"In the swamp," Great-Uncle Daschell corrects him. "If you're really serious about retrieving it, you'll round up your crew and start digging."

Exhausted from all this public speaking, Great-Uncle Daschell collapses into an armchair and asks his grand-niece to fix him a drink.

"And not too much water," he warns. "You don't want to drown it."

Jenny finds herself feeling sorry for her elderly relative, what with all his afflictions, such as drinking, and smoking, and creaky knees, and cataracts, and forgetting, which is a lot like cataracts.

Cataracts are a clouding of the corneas, the lenses of the eyeballs. Left untreated, they become darker and darker until the light goes out. Great-Uncle Daschell's once superior brain is operating in much the same way, starting with a clouding of his short-term memory, and, it could also be argued, his judgment.

None of these afflictions is Daschell Potts's fault—not really—not even the ones that involve personal choice. For Daschell Potts, Jenny knows, is a victim of fate, as we all are.

The kid who can't throw a baseball.

The kid with the big nose.

The kid with floppy ears.

The kid with boring parents.

The kid who grew up on a pirate ship.

And so on.

Maybe you can do something about it and maybe you can't, she muses, *but it's not your fault.*

Before she leaves she gives the old man a hug.

LAND HO!

THE REMNANTS of Coop DeVille's crew are hanging out at a rustic little reggae bar known as the Torn Tailfin. Situated on the Kansas-by-the-Sea inlet directly opposite the famous red lighthouse, the Tailfin, as the locals call it, is the site of many a tall tale and many a fistfight.

The jukebox is playing a country song made famous by Miranda Lambert and covered in this version by the international pop group French Asparagus.

"I used to think about you all the time
I couldn't get you out of my mind
I've still got a long way to go
But I'm doing better
'Cause last time I saw you was two dreams ago."

DeVille's seafaring chums insist that he sit down with them on the open-air patio and pass the grog as they sing the chorus together.

"Two dreams ago
Two dreams ago
I haven't loved you
Since two dreams ago."

As the familiar tune continues, the *Reprehensible*'s former crew members recount their new lives as landlubbers.

Henry, for example, is proud to announce that he works part-time as a Volvo salesman.

"Basically, the cars sell themselves," he explains. "I just have to be well dressed."

"And you are," says Patel, admiringly.

The others tell of equally attractive employment, for in South Florida money is plentiful and no one works very hard.

One of the Knuckleheads is an umbrella unfolder at The Breakers beachfront resort. Queequeg sharpens pencils at the main library of Palm Beach County. Kim Lee is a successful driftwood broker, operating out of a rented warehouse on Ponce de Leon Road. Two-Feather opens and closes the new drawbridge to Palm Beach island, a night job that rarely requires any effort at all. Shawn is a dog walker specializing in purebred Corgis. Jeff, working exclusively with stolen goods, runs a jewelry store on famous Worth Avenue.

All in all, DeVille's men are enjoying the good life for which South Florida is so famous.

"I freak when someone speaks your name
My broken heart will never be the same
They say time heals much more than we know
And last time I saw you was two dreams ago."

110

Two dreams ago
Two dreams ago
I haven't loved you
Since two dreams ago."

By now, all the pirates, including Captain Cooper DeVille, are bawling like babies into their lukewarm beer.

Some songs are like that, ones we hate to remember but are impossible to forget.

Ironically, the lyrics were penned by none other than Daschell Potts during the years when he was trying to make a name for himself on Nashville's Music Row. The music for "Two Dreams Ago" was provided by Mary Jessica Cortez, an intern at the now-defunct Omigod Records who is now quietly keeping company with the heir to the immense Bacardi rum fortune.

But Daschell Potts's songwriting attempts have nothing much to do with the present story.

In fact to a pirate, there is no music that can compare to the siren song of free and lawless living on the high seas.

"Boys," Coop announces, "I've finally located the treasure. The ship is within days of being repaired. Soon there will be nothing to stop us. What say you all? Are you with me?"

With a vocabulary not all that advanced from ancient Ugiri-Tom, the gang responds with a mutual "Huzzah!," which Cooper correctly interprets to be in the affirmative.

"All right, then," he reacts happily. "Let's raise the Jolly Roger and do what we do best."

Henry offers to drive them to Daschell Potts's house in his new Volvo S60, a demo, but since it only seats five he has to make three trips, after which it's off to The Home Depot for picks and shovels.

Within twenty-four hours, Daschell Potts's government-provided house is teeming with activity. To Jenny's surprise and delight, Burson decides to stick around to help out.

There are a number of problems associated with having pirates in your home that few people consider—and Daschell Potts finds himself among this uninformed majority—foremost of which is that pirates expect you to feed them, and as a group they are a notoriously hungry lot.

Burson volunteers himself as chef, a much bigger job than he expects. When DeVille's men aren't tracking in mud from the swamp, they are consuming the equivalent of a baked ham, six roasted chickens, a gallon of coleslaw, and keg of beer a day. Burson hasn't worked this hard since the cleanup following Hurricane Schlemiel.

Across the street, the scene at Potts's house commands increasing attention.

"Didn't I tell you?" insists Professor Dr. Dell-Finian to his colleagues, Professors Von Heron and Dr. Birch. "They are definitely up to something."

Other, bigger issues soon arise.

Daschell Potts's interest in the statue has to do with its presumed Ugiri-Tom runes. He envisions himself spending his twilight years deciphering these mysterious markings in uninterrupted bliss, imagining a special humidity-controlled room in the main building of the university for the statue's permanent placement for study, and a handsome grant from some national endowment for ancient history, to boot.

The pirates, on the other hand, of whom roughly a baker's dozen remain loyal to Coop DeVille, are after treasure, pure and simple, and they don't care how they get it.

Jenny has the intellectual ability to understand both sides, but given her propensity for adventure, when crunch time finally comes, genetic similarities aside, she is likely to side with the pirates. At sixteen, she's already spent plenty of time in classrooms.

Naturally, the pirates are making a mess of the swamp, which is saying something, since swamps are pretty messy places to begin with. Encounters with alligators are commonplace, usually ending with the alligators wisely backing off.

"I was wondering," Jenny says to DeVille, as Burson delivers a pitcher of cold lemonade to the crew. "Shouldn't we have a permit for all this digging? This is an environmentally sensitive area."

"No, that would be impossible," DeVille replies. "Even if we could get a permit, then what we're doing would be legal, and if what we're doing were legal, then we'd be just ordinary workmen, not pirates. Where's the fun in that?"

"Oh," Jenny says, nodding. "I see."

Each day produces cries of "I've found it!" followed by frantic digging, and then a group expression of "Argh!" as an old rusty washing machine is uncovered, or a window air conditioner, or a tractor seat, or a full set of bald tires from a Chrysler LeBaron convertible.

"I thought this was supposed to be pristine wilderness," Jenny remarks as DeVille hauls up yet another soggy roll of worn polyester carpeting to be placed on the growing pile of junk beside Daschell Potts's house.

"It may have started out that way," DeVille says, sweating through his FRENCH ASPARAGUS concert souvenir T-shirt that Jenny gave him as a token of her growing affection, "but now it's just South Florida."

Work stops for a day out of respect for one of the two Kim

Lees, who was dramatically unsuccessful in facing down a particularly large and angry alligator. The surviving pirates use this time to deal with their calluses, cuts, scrapes, snakebites, spider bites, mosquito bites, ant bites, ax accidents, poison toad encounters, poison plant encounters, and to consume all of Jenny's great-uncle's whiskey, which, as has been indicated, is a whole lot.

This last infraction so upsets the old man that he moves into a hotel and washes his hands of the entire disgraceful episode.

"Wake me when it's over," he instructs his grand-niece.

Officially, this leaves Jenny in charge, at least of the premises. Burson signs on as her lieutenant. DeVille retains control of the operation. But since the operation is dependent upon the cooperation of the management, DeVille tends to consult Jenny and Burson on the really big issues.

"I think we may be just digging blindly," he confesses. "Let's take one more look at the map."

Of course, by now the map is so soiled with burned calamari and discolored cooking oil that it is hard to make out anything at all. Lines that could have been cracks in rocks or creeks in swamps or snakes in the sea crisscross one another seemingly at random.

Ugiri-Tom runes depicting dolphins, coral, palm trees, octopi, canoes, women, sea stars, sea cucumbers, and sea celery are dotted here and there like decorations on a birthday cake. To Jenny's untrained eye, it makes no sense at all.

"This could be a giant hoax perpetrated by the Ugiri-Tom," Jenny suggests. "You know, to throw the pirates off the trail?"

"Yeah, why not?" Burson adds. "These were turtle people."

"Well," DeVille responds, surveying an area that looks like

a cross between a United States Air Force bombing practice field and a phosphate mine, "in that case, it's working."

"I wish I could figure out what this means," Jenny says, pointing to a flower-shaped object inside what could be a hat or possibly a turtle shell.

"Where?" DeVille asks.

"Right there," she replies. "Where I'm pointing."

"I could see where you're pointing a lot better if you weren't shining that light in my eyes," DeVille responds, annoyed.

"I'm not shining a light in your eyes," she corrects him. "You're just not looking."

"Well, somebody is shining a light in my eyes," DeVille snaps, looking first at Burson, then up into the trees just in time to see a crow fly off with a piece of broken mirror.

"Well, I'll be," Jenny says. "I've heard they like shiny objects."

The big black bird alights some distance away, high in the twisted branches of a weathered ficus tree, the piece of mirror clasped securely in his long, sharp beak. Of a breed among nature's cleverer animals, this particular raven seems especially pleased with himself.

Wisely, lest he drop his prize to the ground, he suppresses the instinct to crow over his achievement.

"Look," DeVille announces, "there are more pieces of mirror on the ground."

He kneels down to pick up a sliver.

"Don't cut yourself," Jenny warns.

"I'm not worried about that," DeVille replies in a near whisper. "This isn't a broken mirror."

Jenny kneels beside him. Her lightly sweet perfume meets

with the musky aroma of his pirate sweat like two weather systems colliding over the Rockies.

The result is a lot like lightning.

For a moment (or is it an eternity?) neither teen moves, neither teen breathes.

Piracy? Try chemistry.

Gingerly, as if it might crumble into dust in a light breeze, DeVille presents the iridescent object to Jenny Snow.

No bigger than a human thumbnail, it is carved with a tiny rune that resembles a flower inside a hat.

"Holy shark bait!" Jenny exclaims. "It's a fragment from the Ugiri-Tom statue."

"So it would seem," DeVille agrees. "And look, here's more."

To Jenny's astonishment, scattered around the edge of one of the more or less randomly situated holes are hundreds, perhaps thousands, of tiny shards of shiny pearlescent shell, many bearing ancient markings.

"No wonder we couldn't find it," Jenny observes. "We've been looking for a seventeen-foot statue, not the site of a million little pieces."

It is likely that we will never know who broke the Ugiri-Tom statue. Perhaps the first cracks occurred when the sacred object was first lashed to the outrigger canoes piloted by the Ugiri-Tom twins, Tak-Me and Tak-Ma, panicked and pursued by cannonballs whizzing over their heads and smashing into beach rock.

Or maybe it was an unlucky fleeing foot striking a mangrove root centuries ago that caused the oversize artifact to take a disastrous tumble against a sleeping gopher tortoise in the swamp.

If not that, then possibly it was the energetic activity of alligators over the succeeding years, snorting and rooting and thrashing about in the mud to form the perfect wallows. It's not at all unusual for one of these ancient reptiles to top off at eight hundred pounds. Imagine what an entire neighborhood of them might do.

But the likeliest explanation for the destruction of the statue is the one DeVille hates most to contemplate. Not unlike the circumstances that caused the recent obliteration of the Ugiri-Tom treasure map, the smithereening of the Ugiri-Tom statue could very well have the result of active human stupidity: the ham-handed clumsiness of DeVille's own loutish men.

Untrained in archaeological techniques, they simply decided to dig wherever the digging looked promising (or easy), not entirely certain of what they were looking for but anticipating that it would be a great big priceless statue standing upright and shining like the sun.

What oafs! thinks DeVille. *They couldn't hunt for Easter eggs without breaking them to bits.*

DeVille sends his crew back to the Torn Tailfin to await further instructions, all but Queequeg, with his experience in coffin making, Patel, whose embroidery has recently impressed the captain, and Curly, who has demonstrated a certain aptitude for weaving.

These skills, DeVille knows, will come in handy.

In the kitchen, Burson, grateful for the reduced workload, quickly switches the menu to grilled cheese sandwiches.

"Patel, Curly, and Ruthless," DeVille orders decisively, "you use your delicate touch to gather up all the broken pieces from the ground. Queequeg, you build a soft-lined, airtight box to put them in. I'll go in search of that thieving crow and recover whatever he may have stolen."

"And I'll go borrow one of my mother's glue guns," Jenny volunteers.

"Excellent idea," DeVille replies. "Come hell or high water, we're going to put this statue back together the way it was."

But despite the confidence exhibited in the young pirate's voice, in his heart he knows it is only bravado, feigned leadership performed for a tender audience of one: Jenny Snow.

It is, he knows deep down, much ado about nothing.

As Captain Cooper DeVille gazes at the fragmented disaster glinting in the mud at his feet like the site of a boatload of recently offloaded and scaled mackerel filets, he says out loud, "That Ugiri-Tom totem is a goner."

THE STATUE FACTORY

ALTHOUGH GREAT-UNCLE DASCHELL is out living the life of Riley in a nearby Palm Beach hotel, his house is a hive of activity, with an amateur artifact restoration team working long into the night.

Curly and Patel deliver shiny totem shards in plastic Wal-Mart bags they find stuck in trees and fences, wash the pieces carefully in the kitchen sink, and lay them out on the kitchen table, where Jenny and DeVille examine them for possible matches.

Burson, a good, kind, and reliable young man, mindful of his responsibilities at the South Florida Loggerhead Turtle Rehabilitation Center, and not wishing to worry his parents, goes home for dinner and a good night's sleep.

"He'll be back," Jenny predicts to DeVille. "That's just his way."

When Jenny and DeVille find two pieces of totem shard that fit together, which occasionally happens, Jenny attaches them with the glue gun she borrowed, without asking, from her mother.

It is a tedious process.

"Wouldn't this go faster if we got somebody who knows what he or she is doing?" Jenny asks her partner.

"An expert in this line of work would turn us in to the authorities," DeVille explains. "Not only would we lose the treasure, we'd lose our freedom. A pirate must be ever vigilant. That's why there's always somebody assigned to the crow's nest."

"The what?" Jenny responds, thinking of the big black bird that found the first shard.

"The washtub-like object nailed to the top of the mainmast," Cooper explains. "It's a very important job."

Jenny sighs.

"Well," she says, more or less to herself, "I guess it's really no more complicated than assembling a jigsaw puzzle, only with lots more pieces, three dimensions, extra parts, and no picture on the box."

"That's the spirit," DeVille says encouragingly.

"Freaking-A," agrees the language-challenged Ruthless.

"Excuse me, Captain," Queequeg interrupts. "It's about the dimensions of the container. It's to hold a seventeen-foot loggerhead turtle statue, yes?"

"Correct," DeVille says.

Queequeg whistles.

"That be some big box," Queequeg observes. "Close to twenty feet long. Who's going to carry that big box to the ship?"

"One storm at a time, Queequeg," DeVille cautions. "One storm at a time."

"Okay, boss," Queequeg replies, as the wood shavings curl up in soft piles at his feet. "Whatever you say."

Day and night, the operation continues until after a week, fully one-third of a brilliant, beautiful, serrated, leaf-shaped turtle carapace and a single, gracefully curved turtle foot are formed out of the pulverized pearlescent pickings plucked from the swamp behind Daschell Potts's government-provided house.

As has been pointed out, Daschell Potts has lived a long, colorful, and controversial life, jumping from one interesting profession to another.

Now he is spending his final years enjoying the largesse of a government that values his well-honed encryption skills.

Such a man does not arrive at the end of his days without making a few enemies along the way, and Potts certainly has his share. Most recently, he is the object of scrutiny among three recently hired professors of the Florida Atlantic University in Kansas-by-the-Sea.

This cliquish group considers Daschell Potts a freeloader if not an outright fraud. They deeply resent his cushy setup for what from their perspective is no work whatsoever (although how one can tell in South Florida whether a person is working or not is hard to imagine), and they are also in regular email contact with a certain branch of the United States government whose primary interest is in collecting taxes on selected individuals' financial windfalls.

The observation post of the three busybodies consists of cramped and cluttered offices in the seven-story building on the other side of the road.

"What can he be doing with all those people in the swamp?" Professor Dr. Dell-Finian asks his colleague Professor Dr. Von Heron.

"Yes, and why was that one fellow carried out in an ambulance?" chimed in Professor Dr. Lucius Birch, BA, MA, PhD, DD, JD, MD, and OBE. "He appeared to be the victim of an alligator attack."

Each day, all three have their faces pressed against the windows on the fifth floor, leaving oily smudge marks where their big noses come in contact with the glass.

Instead of brewing coffee in the professors' lounge, working diligently on the subjects of their own lucrative government grants, these three jealous snoops are busy brewing trouble for Daschell Potts and, by extension, his grand-niece, her boyfriends, and all their riffraff pals.

The three nosy professors have seen enough.

More accurately, they have not seen enough to know what's going on, but they've seen enough to arouse their suspicions that whatever is going on should be stopped.

In many respects, they resemble the appointed officials of a suburban homes association.

Brazenly, they rap on Daschell Potts's front door.

Opening the door just a crack, Jenny answers, "Yes?" meaning, of course, "Go away."

"We are colleagues of Professor Potts's," Professor Dr. Dell-Finian announces in his most unctuous and officious manner—a repelling way to begin a conversation with anyone, but especially insulting to a young girl of Jenny's intelligence and self-confidence. "Take us to him."

"You'd never fit on my Vespa," Jenny replies. "We'd have to make six trips. Three for you guys. Three more for your noses."

She shuts the door in their faces.

"Well, I never," blusters Professor Dr. Birch, who declares in a threatening if somewhat difficult to understand accent, "You haven't seen the last of us, little lady."

"Okay by me," Jenny calls out. "Just don't let the hut shadow strike your posterior on the way out."

Jenny goes upstairs to dye her hair again. This time she

chooses an Irish red with highlights of light purple on either side of her symmetrical face. Delighted with the outcome, she seeks out Cooper for what she is certain will be his enthusiastic approval.

But DeVille is in no mood to admire Jenny's beauty, however surprising and store-bought it may be.

"We've got to get out of here," DeVille warns her.

"But I was just going out for pizzas," Jenny protests.

"Those people who were at the door," DeVille continues. "They're on to us. Trust me, a pirate can tell when it's time to set sail."

"But what about the statue?" Jenny asks. "Surely we're not abandoning that."

"Queequeg has finished the container," DeVille reports. "Curly, Patel, and Ruthless have recovered all the pieces from the swamp. We'll toss everything into the box and take it to the ship. We can continue to work on it at sea."

"It's easy to see that you've never used a glue gun," Jenny complains. "They're tricky enough when your furniture is standing still, but bouncing up and down on the waves? I don't think you're going to be happy with the outcome."

"We have no choice," DeVille says. "They could be back with the cops at any minute."

As he speaks, a car with a flashing red hood-mounted light pulls into the driveway.

"Uh-oh," says Jenny, giving her hair a provocative shake, "looks like we're too late."

Attracted by the flashing red light, which makes her heart pound with fear, Jenny races to the window, arriving at the same moment at the ever-alert African gray parrot, Ruthless.

Together, they witness the arrival of not a squadron of

Kansas-by-the-Sea police cruisers but a single black vintage stretch limousine hearse with a portable red warning light suction-cupped on top.

When the door on the driver's side opens, the long, lanky frame of Queequeg unfolds itself in the driveway like a fine pocketknife.

"Holy shark bait!" Jenny remarks.

"Bet sweet do-danga!" agrees the parrot.

"We need something that can haul an extra-long coffin without arousing suspicion," DeVille explains.

"How does an eighteen-foot coffin fail to arouse suspicion?" Jenny asks. "Are there a lot of seventeen-foot-tall people dying in Florida?"

"Not to my knowledge," admits Deville, "but two six-footers and a somewhat shrunken grandmother laid-end-to-end might fit. Let's assume for a moment that they all died in a home appliance nuclear accident."

"Let's not," Jenny counters. "Anyway, stick to your story if you must. I prefer to follow on my Vespa."

DeVille is right about one thing. Big cars do not attract attention in South Florida.

Everywhere you look someone is driving a car that's bigger, better, fancier, more outlandish, and just plain more expensive than the one ahead of it. So when the little motorcade makes a quick stop at the Torn Tailfin to pick up the motley remnants of the *Reprehensible*'s crew to take to the shipyard in Riviera Beach, not a single customer bothers to look up from his margarita, daiquiri, or flat Corona beer, and as if Cooper had never left, the jukebox wails on, "Oh how I loved you, truly loved you, but that was two dreams ago."

As far as these people are concerned, it's just another day

in paradise, an assessment shared by the Kansas-by-the-Sea law enforcement authorities, who, having been anonymously alerted by a whispering caller referring to himself only as Professor Dr. Nobody Special, "just an average guy," leave the absent Daschell Potts a warning note on his front door to clean up his backyard within ninety days or face a possible fine of forty dollars, not to mention a public citation of non-compliance from the Possum Wood Homes Association.

On returning home from the posh comforts of his Palm Beach hotel, Potts throws the official admonition into the recycling bin, along with the many offers for magazine subscriptions, credit cards, investment seminars, and not-for-profit memberships that accumulated while he was out. He keeps the ones that include free self-adhesive return address labels.

He is pleased to discover that Jenny has left him one of Burson's delicious chicken pies in the fridge.

After so much pampering at that hotel, Daschell Potts thinks, *it's good to be back where things are normal.*

When the Norwegians settled Minnesota, they did so because it seemed to them to have the attributes of Norway, without Norway's flaws.

The settlers of Kansas-by-the-Sea were similarly motivated.

If you were to get into your car in the town of Kansas-by-the-Sea with the goal of traveling to Kansas, the real Kansas, the one that became a state at the end of the War Between the States in 1865, you would travel north and west for a while on crowded Florida highways, with most of the cars headed in the opposite direction toward the theme parks in the north-central part of the state, where previously there was little more than lizards, brush, and free oranges.

Most of the people would be expecting to have the time of their lives, but we know that by the time they return home they will be considerably disappointed by the long lines, high prices, and costumed characters.

At some point, you cross the Florida state line into Georgia, with the option of continuing into Alabama, where you'll see plenty of red dirt and peanut farms, or, if you prefer, the state of Tennessee.

Should you choose the Tennessee route, you'll see some very nice mountains, in which many people eke out a living fixing one another's cars.

Eventually you will cross a river into Kentucky and sometime after that catch a high-speed glimpse of the famed Saint Louis arch as you enter Missouri.

You still have a long way to go, and I'm sorry to report that it's on one of the most boring stretches of highway in the world, but hang in there, because once you traverse Missouri, after some one thousand and six hundred miles recorded on your automobile's odometer—assuming you don't succumb to the enticement of side trips to the Jack Daniel's distillery or Dollywood or the Oak Ridge nuclear complex—and three excruciating days of relentless and dangerous driving, you will find yourself in the state of Kansas, wishing you had never left Florida in the first place.

At this particular moment you will feel like a Norwegian wandering aimlessly in Minnesota's expansive city suburbs, with many doubts, second thoughts, and a lifetime of buyer's remorse.

Each of us is lost.

This is the human condition.

One way to deal with this pervasive existential issue, however, is to assign a familiar name to wherever it is you happen to be.

Thus, geography is littered with place names such as New England, New York, New Jersey, New Bedford, New Brunswick, New Caledonia, New Delhi, New Guinea, New Hampshire, New Haven, New Orleans, New Madrid, New Mexico, and Kansas-by-the-Sea, among countless others.

Interestingly (perhaps), the motto of the city of Kansas-by-the-Sea is the single memorable word, "Someday."

Since there resides within us a gene that says, in effect, "I gotta get outta this place," even if our wisest ancestors have searched the world over and determined that where we are is the best possible place to be, a person born and raised in Kansas-by-the-Sea will likely respond by asking, "Is this all there is?"

Thus, Jenny's willingness to ship out once again on the *Reprehensible* is easy to understand. With a treasure in tow, and at least one boyfriend more or less under control, she trusts in the notion of the wind at one's back being a benevolent force.

That she is naïve is a given.

In addition to all of us being lost, we are also naïve to a greater or lesser degree, with death, possibly, offering the only cure for that affliction.

(But who knows? Maybe not.)

Although the pirates do not know it at the time, the three envious professors from Florida Atlantic University are after them.

Shamelessly, and quite illegally, the jealous academics break into Potts's house while he is, shall we say, "sleeping" under the influence of alcoholic beverages, and, finding the calamari-stained map, soak it in a solution of Kava-Lava ink restorative, a concoction of their own secret and brilliant creation, and conclude that someone has recently looted a valuable Ugiri-Tom treasure right from under their enormous noses.

This infuriates them to a man.

Excitedly, they cite international treaties, high-level multicultural summits, presidential promises, congressional resolutions, and business deals hammered out between themselves and major American corporations.

They vow to set things straight, which, in their minds means to get the treasure "for the benefit of those who most deserve to benefit," which is another way of saying to get it for themselves.

"This could be as big a find as the Dead Sea Scrolls," announces Professor Dr. Birch.

"It could easily rival the discovery of the Gospel of Judas," agrees Professor Dr. Dell-Finian.

"It's certainly as big a find as that woodpecker in Arkansas," Professor Dr. Von Heron observes. "You know, the one that everybody thought was extinct? It looks like that cartoon character, what's-his-name?"

The other two professors look at Professor Dr. Von Heron with contempt. Although not truly a stupid man, he is always saying something stupid, which, as far as the other two professors are concerned, is just as bad.

"No one has actually seen that woodpecker," Professor Dr. Dell-Finian points out.

"Yes, they have," Professor Dr. Von Heron replies.

"No, they haven't," insists Professor Dr. Dell-Finian.

"But, there are photographs . . ." Professor Dr. Von Heron begins, but Professor Dr. Birch holds up his hand like a traffic cop in Paris, France, and that puts an immediate stop to the argument.

While the *Reprehensible* is being loaded with provisions, Jenny writes a long and long-overdue letter to her parents.

In it, she thanks them for the many freedoms they have afforded her over the years, including the gift of her beloved Vespa, which she is presently sending home with Queequeg in the back of the stretch limo for safekeeping; she thanks her father for conveying to her that truth is an elusive thing requiring constant pursuit and correction; she thanks her mother for her artistic gifts, and admits to borrowing a glue gun; so her parents won't worry needlessly, Jenny explains that she had taken a summer job aboard a cruise ship as an art restorer, that she will send letters from every port, and that she will be back in time for school in mid-August. And of course she adds that she loves them, which, for all their benign faults, she truly does.

As it turns out, this news is not the great shock that it might have been under other circumstances. Only the day before, Jenny's parents learn that they've won a tidy sum in the Florida State "Pick Three" lottery, and to celebrate, decide to take a second honeymoon, a cruise on the next available sailing, which turns out to be a newly refurbished vessel called the *Royal Kansan* that leaves from Fort Lauderdale on a romantic tour of the Bermuda Triangle.

The Snows arrange for a housekeeper, a stout, no-nonsense Canadian woman named Mrs. Flog, whose son once wrote a book about a household nuclear accident, to look after Jenny and the backyard flowers.

Mrs. Flog has met none of the Snows. All arrangements were made at the last minute through a commercial house-and-child-sitting service called Squatter's Rights.

Mrs. Flog does a grand job with the garden but wonders if the part about the teenage girl is some sort of test of her qualifications, inasmuch as there is no girl around.

Americans! Mrs. Flog thinks.

RETURN TO THE SEA

BURSON SURPRISES HIMSELF.

Just as the *Reprehensible* weighs anchor, its precious cargo rattling like a box of broken seashells in the hold, he leaps from the pier and tumbles like a hedgehog across the deck, where he comes to a rest at Jenny's canvas-covered feet.

"OOOF!" announces Burson.

"Fancy meeting you here," Jenny says with a self-conscious giggle as Burson attempts to catch his breath.

From the upper deck, Captain Coop DeVille watches the pair of youngsters with unblinking eyes.

Still gasping, Burson explains, "I didn't want to miss anything."

Once out of sight of land, DeVille orders the Ugiri-Tom loggerhead turtle totem reconstruction production line reestablished as quickly as possible. He sends Patel up to the crow's nest to keep a sharp eye out for pursuers. He assigns Kim Lee (which one remains unknown) to keep a sharp eye on Jenny and Burson.

Luckily for the agile, rope-climbing Patel, who is easily bored gazing out at the endless, empty sea, a library book was left behind in the high-flying tub: *Ka-blam! The True Story of a*

Household Nuclear Explosion by Luger Flog, translated from Canadian English into American English by Daschell Potts.

This looks interesting, Patel says to himself.

(We, of course, know otherwise.)

Soon, and understandably, Patel is fast asleep, dreaming of turtles.

Far below, Jenny and her glue gun are back in the thick of it. Although she has the unexpected but appreciated assistance of the easygoing Burson, she finds her task hampered by a number of unforeseen factors.

First of all, eighteenth-century pirate ships are fundamentally compact vessels that don't easily permit a twenty-foot room for glue gun work. Several staterooms are removed, which does not please their former inhabitants, specifically the surviving Kim Lee, Jeff, Larry, Two-Feather, and Shawn, who find themselves bunking together in a room no bigger than nine by nine (not as big as the elevator in the tiny but trendy South Beach Rio Tostada Hotel) in which they share a single towel.

"Argh!" they say to anyone inclined to listen.

DeVille reminds them that hardship at sea goes without saying. He also reminds them that he has the absolute authority to throw any one of them overboard.

The grousing immediately stops.

Jenny faces other challenges. She and Burson discover that the digging crew, in their enthusiasm, unearthed a lot more statue parts. Many shiny objects in Queequeg's box obviously do not belong to the Ugiri-Tom totem. For example, there are dog tags, dimes, toe rings, nose and navel piercings, car keys, zipper pulls, sharks' teeth, granola bar wrappers, lug bolts, and half a dozen diamond engagement rings.

Jenny sets these items aside in case they may be needed later on.

Another difficulty, one that she predicted, is the rise and fall of the *Reprehensible* on the waves of the Atlantic Ocean. This constant undulation forces Jenny to do much of her work over again, which not only wastes glue but also results in a front foot being affixed as a back foot.

She and Burson agree: the working conditions are terribly frustrating, but to their everlasting credit, they persevere.

Meanwhile, Captain Cooper DeVille, direct descendant of Edward Teach, understudy to Captain Kidd, Scourge of the Seven Seas, and the man later known to history as the notorious Blackbeard, who once shot a man in Reno just to see him die, is properly preoccupied with managerial matters. Some sort of seacraft is apparently in pursuit of the *Reprehensible*.

"Patel," he shouts. "What see you?"

From the crow's nest comes a sound like that of thick-and-shiny-pelted beavers lazily gnawing on tender saplings in the spring.

"Wake up, you worthless scalawag!" shouts DeVille.

He unfolds his spyglass and locks in on the approaching craft.

Using resources provided by the United States government, the three "professors" have chartered a vessel of dubious speed and seaworthiness for their own purposes.

More experienced sailors would recognize the ship as a garbage scow recently decommissioned by the City of Miami Beach, but these learned men, for all their years of alleged superior academic training, believe it to be a chase boat formerly operated by the United States Coast Guard. The pervasive fetid odor it emits they dismiss as that of the leftover sweat of hard-working young men in crisp white uniforms.

The man who rents it to them, a weasely scoundrel known throughout the region as Wehrman the German (coincidentally, he is also the owner of *Corrections* magazine), insists on a cash deposit of three thousand dollars, plus an ironclad contract calling for another twelve thousand dollars should the boat fail to be returned by the predetermined date, some six days hence, a sum that the three foolhardy professors promptly pay (inasmuch as it's not *their* money). Indeed, they sign the agreement with no more examination than they might give to a student requesting a hall pass.

Smart and stupid. Two sides of the same coin.

It's hard to say who has the least maneuverable ship. The garbage scow is built to sit low in the water, much like a river barge, and turning it all the way around can take hours in a strong current. On the other hand, an old three-masted square-rigger flying the Jolly Roger is clunky too, compared to sleek modern ships with their mighty engines, especially given that the *Reprehensible* is, at present, short-handed.

Evasion, then, is ineffective. Collision seems the far more likely outcome.

Professors Drs. Birch, Dell-Finian, and Von Heron, dressed in white lab coats and Windsor-knotted ties, puff themselves up like ancient dodos from Mauritius, demanding attention.

"Halt!" the panicked pursuers command from their free-floating trash bin. "Halt in the name of righteous curiosity!"

Who are these guys? DeVille asks himself. *And what do they want with me?*

Meanwhile, Jenny is in her lab with Burson, where they are laboring to restore the massive Ugiri-Tom artifact. What she lacks in training she makes up for in pursuit of perfection. To this end, she finds Burson to be a soothing influence, compared to the restless—even jumpy—Coop DeVille.

Only when a piece obviously is missing altogether does she consult with Burson about the substitution of a safe-deposit box key, a glass eyeball, a casino token, or a hearing aid battery, all of which are among the more commonly found objects amid the swamps, golf courses, parking lots, and beaches of South Florida.

The ever-dependable Henry is supervising the preparation of the meals, which, while consisting largely of fish dishes, are quite wonderful, in Jenny's opinion, except for the squid, which she always declines. These she delivers to the lab workers at regular intervals.

In the sea, well outside the illusory protection of the Ugiri-Tom totem restoration lab, the three professors resort to throwing chunks of unidentifiable garbage at the side of the *Reprehensible*. These bounce off with a soft thud, then splash into the water, where they are immediately set upon by unseen but perpetually hungry creatures.

"Now we're getting somewhere," Professor Dr. Birch observes, while Professor Dr. Dell-Finian prays for a safe return to land and Professor Dr. Von Heron throws up into the churning waters, attracting even more marine creatures to the unexpected bounty.

That the three professors have no plan seems not to occur to them. They are driven solely by their sense of outrage.

Alas, even with right on your side, fortune favors whomever she deems, the prepared mind and the ignorant soul alike, so it isn't long before the three professors discover that their role is not to be that of conquerors, rescuers, or heroes but is limited solely to that of amazed eyewitnesses.

Are they to shout at the pirates? Throw stones at them? Threaten to inform the authorities?

No.

They are merely persons who accidentally chance upon the scene. For it is Professor Dr. Birch, Professor Dr. Dell-Finian, and Professor Dr. Von Heron who find themselves in the remarkable position to recount the rest of the story.

Oh, not all of it, of course. They can't see inside the stateroom where Captain Cooper DeVille has dropped to one knee to present a gold object to his beloved.

"This locket has been in my family for many generations," he tells Jennifer in his most sincere-sounding voice. "Inside is contained a coiled strand of the beard of the famous pirate Blackbeard, my direct ancestor. I offer it to you now as a token of the riches yet to come."

Jenny is gluing the last piece of turtle pearl into place.

"You're full of barge bilge," she tells DeVille. "Help me get this statue back into Queequeg's coffin," she orders him.

"What do you mean 'full of barge bilge'?" DeVille replies, his feelings bruised.

"I mean, you ninny," she says, "that that's the very locket you stole from my house, and that hair inside is no more a pirate's whisker than I'm the queen of the Ugiri-Tom."

"Oops!" says DeVille.

"Really!" says Jenny. "The nerve of some people."

"It's an honest mistake," DeVille avows.

"Coop, it is a *dis*honest mistake," Jenny corrects him with a sigh. "It's the pirate in you, I suppose."

Despite his pitiful effort at deception, she hugs him.

"Oh, Jenny," DeVille says, his heart melting.

It is at that moment that the *Reprehensible* strikes the iceberg, a blow that sends the timbers rattling from stem to stern, topples the foremast and mizzenmast like matchsticks, leaving only the mainmast standing like a lonesome pine, and tearing a thirty-foot gash in the hold.

The gold locket that Coop DeVille purloined from the top dresser drawer in Jenny Snow's bedroom is not only a family heirloom, as has been mentioned, but also a family hair loom, or, at the very least, a tiny family hair repository, for someone in Jenny Snow's distant past owned the wispy strands of hair that are curled so carefully within.

DeVille attempts to change its provenance, but Jenny knows better.

So much separates us from our ancestors. Memories fade. Pictures get lost, or, far worse, misidentified.

How, for example, years later, is one to distinguish between a common next-door neighbor playmate and a full-blooded cross-eyed cousin if no one bothered to label the back of the photo? And baby pictures? Give me a break. All babies look like hamsters, a fact that few families admit.

Some people practice genealogy. They research marriage records, birth records, burial records, and newspaper clippings about the burning of county courthouses in county seats, of which there has been a rash over the centuries.

Nowadays, it seems, the only reliable method for establishing connections to one's relations is through expensive DNA testing, and the fact is, mostly what this laboratory miracle shows is that we're each of us as closely related to field mice as we are to people from Wisconsin.

EEK! A mouse!

Pipe down. It's only your cousin, Lindsay Anne.

But we are neglecting the encounter with the iceberg, a matter of far more immediacy than wispy strands of DNA or old hair, no matter how well preserved.

A DAY TO REMEMBER

FEW MOMENTS in the history of a sailing ship are as devastating as colliding with an iceberg.

At least, the crew of the *Reprehensible* is *assuming* it's an iceberg—in the warm waters of the Caribbean this is not a particularly well-formed assumption, but then, we've already commented on the intellectual capabilities of pirates in general.

Actually, what the *Reprehensible* collides with is the object once known as Turtle Rock, which has been bobbing around in the ocean undetected for several weeks now, ever since it was first sent out to sea by Vanessa Snow's unequalled prowess with a glue gun. As big as a steamroller and twice as sharp, Turtle Rock quickly reduces the starboard side of the *Reprehensible* to splinters.

The three professors, their mouths agape, two from astonishment and one from seasickness, witness the whole thing.

"Floating boulders!" shouts Professor Dr. Birch. "Holy shark bait!"

Few expressions are more apt. As pirates dive overboard, great white sharks circle the gathering debris and dine on the occasional miscreant and scallywag.

As if this is not catastrophic enough, the three professors have a front-row seat to the emergence of a giant squid rising up through the boiling waters of the sinking *Reprehensible* to snatch the last of the Knuckleheads and take him on a one-way trip to Davy Jones's locker where together one of them enjoys a leisurely lunch.

"The horror of that moment I shall never, ever forget," cries Professor Dr. Birch.

"Oh, yes, you will," replies Professor Dr. Dell-Finian, "if you don't make a note of it."

But the garbage scow, while a convenient position from which to view the loss of the *Reprehensible,* likewise is not spared. The whirlpool created by the sinking ship sucks the professors' boat into its swirling vortex, from which it is never seen again, not that anyone would care to.

The professors enjoy a kinder fate. The crow's nest affixed to the top of the mainmast of the *Reprehensible* is the last part of the ship to touch water. Fortuitously, because of poor workmanship, it separates from the mast and floats to a position within reach of three academically honored busybodies, who need no encouragement to clamber aboard.

Rub-a-dub-dub, the three men in a tub bob slowly but safely to shore, where, as common sense would suggest, they disappear into the woodwork, so to speak.

News of the maritime disaster is slow in reaching Kansas-by-the-Sea.

For one thing, the social season is winding down in Palm Beach—the rich are returning to cooler climes—so there are only the bargain-hunting tourist families from England and Germany and Italy occupying the resorts and hotels, and they, understandably, have little interest in calamities befalling Americans.

Anyway, there's a big difference between a report that's headlined "Ship Strikes Rock," which is what the *Palm Beach Post* reports, and one that says "Rock Strikes Ship," which is how *Corrections* magazine more accurately handled it.

In either case, however, it doesn't sound that much out of the ordinary. Now, if it had been "Meteor Strikes Ship," or "Priceless Public Artwork Rips Vintage Pirate Ship Asunder," or "Killer Boulder Threatens Shipping Lanes," well, maybe then you'd have something.

It all depends on how you look at it, and since the only eyewitnesses are the three shaken professors from Florida Atlantic University, who aren't talking, then there isn't much to say.

One reason they aren't talking is for fear of reprisal from the hotheaded chancellor of the university. Another is the rental contract with Wehrman the German, who doubtless will enforce the expensive "unreturned vessel" clause. Finally, they are ashamed that despite being right there on the scene, the best they could do was save their own worthless hides. All the others aboard the *Reprehensible,* they presume, are lost at sea.

With great somberness in a secret ceremony at the corner booth of Wendy's, the professors take a vow of mutual silence.

Among those you might think would be most concerned are Jenny's parents, the Snows, but they're still enjoying their second-honeymoon cruise aboard the *Royal Kansan,* far from the intermittent doses of hysteria that pass for news these days.

Thinking their daughter safe in the competent and loving hands of Mrs. Flog, the Snows have no reason to connect Jenny with the minor wooden ship disaster mentioned by some gossipy old man at the dinner table that evening.

Who rides around the Atlantic in wooden ships these days? Certainly nobody we would know, they think.

Within days—no, to be more accurate, within minutes, life in Kansas-by-the-Sea is back to the way it was. Even this is an exaggeration. The sinking of the *Reprehensible* has absolutely no effect on the residents of, workers in, or visitors to Kansas-by-the-Sea.

Only the absent-minded Daschell Potts pauses to wonder from time to time, before he forgets what he is thinking about and wanders into his kitchen in search of something to eat or drink.

SUPERIOR CRAFTSMANSHIP

IN THE LONG and tragic history of disasters as sea, no vessel of any size compares in seaworthiness to the coffin fashioned by the *Reprehensible*'s Queequeg. As you will discover if you ever chance upon *Antiques Road Show* on PBS, good-quality cabinetmaking stands the test of time.

That said, we should not be surprised to find that Jenny, Cooper, and Burson, at first clinging to the side of the custom-made eighteen-foot Ugiri-Tom totem artifacts container, as wide as a winged goddess of the sea and as swift, sleek, secure, and maneuverable as a narrow punt, soon enough are atop the airtight box all in a row like members of the West Hempstead Country Day School rowing team.

Some things are clearly meant to be.

A sail is handy, of course, given the rough waters the three-some finds themselves in, so for this Jenny salvages the starched white tablecloth from the dining room that Henry prepared for the engagement announcement dinner that, unknown to Jenny (or Burson, for that matter), DeVille ordered prior to his presentation of Jenny's stolen locket.

As for Henry:

Within a few months, his name will again appear engraved on a metal strip glued to a polished walnut plaque hanging on the east wall of the showroom of Palm Beach Volvo, just above the elegant new S90 Turbo. Henry likened the job to working in a library, but with a clientele whose pockets are spilling over with idle cash.

Jenny fixes the sail into place with a succession of sharp splinters from the mizzenmast.

Soon, the sea breezes and currents carry the three comrades to a tiny island, where, ironically, the vanquished race of the Ugiri-Tom once worshiped the winged god of the sea.

Life, at least life for this particular statue, has come full circle.

Jenny's life remains up in the air.

But the air in which it lingers is sweet, and the improvements on the little atoll once occupied by the most qualified members of the Ugiri-Tom include fresh water, banana plants, orange trees, coconut palms, and implements for fishing.

A pocket-size paradise, perhaps, but a paradise nonetheless.

Each morning, the three comrades arise and go about their voluntary duties. Cooper catches fish. Burson cooks. Jenny's time, the boys agree, is best spent repairing the statue.

All in all, it's a good life.

Afternoons are free, and swimming is the most popular sport. On one occasion, DeVille kisses Jenny underwater, a feat, by the way, that can only be pictured, not felt, given the total moisture content of the medium. On another occasion Burson, finding Jenny sunning herself on a rock, summons up the courage to kiss her on her Chap-Sticked lips.

The result is somewhat fishlike, salty and slobbery, but, like sushi, not bad.

When DeVille touches Jenny, it feels like an electric eel, sending electric shock waves all the way to Jenny's painted toes. When Burson places his gentle hand on Jenny's tanned bare arm, it makes her think of comforting caresses from a harbor seal.

A nice, friendly one, with sweet breath.

But still, one island? Two suitors?

Who can ask for anything more?

If we were to hold an election today, Jenny thinks, *there is little doubt who would be named queen.*

As time passes, Jenny puts each boy through a series of tests: who can run the fastest, dive the deepest, tell the funniest story, catch the most sand crabs, sing her the sweetest song.

Meanwhile, thanks to Jenny's skillful labor, the Ugiri-Tom statue takes shape, piece by piece, glue glob by glue glob. Eventually, the day arrives when it is fully restored, except for a few missing parts for which common objects have been substituted, rising to an astonishing height of seventeen feet, shining like a galactic telescope mirror in the warm Caribbean sun.

By now, the crowd of "Three's Company" is comfortable with the arrangements. DeVille loves Jenny. Burson loves Jenny. Jenny loves Burson and DeVille each in different ways, for different reasons. DeVille and Burson are friends. Everybody behaves.

No one dares to break the spell.

As all those reggae and calypso songs suggest, life is laidback and easygoing down by the sea.

In fact, life is so nice on the atoll that Jenny finds herself more than a little annoyed when an insomniac codger who, at the last minute booked passage on the *Royal Kansan,* spots her shiny, repaired, and re-erected loggerhead effigy in the Caribbean moonlight and persuades the Norwegian captain, a hard-working fellow named Sven Svenson, to dispatch a lifeboat to investigate.

Jenny's parents are disconcerted too to learn that their second honeymoon has come to a crashing conclusion. Now, through no fault of their own, they must make room for three extra chairs at their table.

Cripes, Mr. Snow thinks, *you can't move your elbow far enough to reach that little dish of iced butter.*

Oh, well, thinks his wife, *at least it's still all you can eat.*

"Please pass the marmalade," she asks DeVille, who knocks over a pitcher of tea in the process.

"Dang!" shouts Jenny's father. "I look like I've peed in my pants."

Hovering nearby, Captain Svenson says, "I would join you folks for dessert, but it looks as if you're a bit overcrowded. Perhaps at breakfast, yes?"

"Captain?" says DeVille, standing up with an outstretched hand. "Permit me to introduce myself. I am Cooper DeVille, also a ship's captain, although presently sans command."

"*The* Captain DeVille?" Captain Svenson asks, clearly impressed.

"I know of no others," DeVille replies.

Cruise ships are among mankind's more space-saving inventions, ranking second only to spaceships, space stations, and middle-schoolers' lockers. No matter how big they appear when seen from the outside, such as when docked in Puerto Dingo, or on a color calendar depicting half-dressed young people frolicking on the lido deck, inside they are warrens of tiny cubicles and hidey-holes. You would be forgiven for suspecting that their designers were a race of intellectually advanced prairie dogs.

Thus, the only way to get the massive Ugiri-Tom totem on board the *Royal Kansan* is to remove an equal amount of material. Think of it as a glass of water. If this much is going in, that much is going out.

It's called displacement.

Recognizing that the mother-of-pearl statue is much too valuable to be sitting out in the middle of nowhere, where thieves break in and steal and moth and rust doth corrupt, the captain orders that an equivalent amount of luggage be removed from the ship and left on the Ugiri-Tom's sacred island.

Understandably, certain people object, namely those whose luggage is being offloaded even as they complain. But in the captain's mind, it is all for the greater good—he is the captain, after all, conferred with the authority of a monarch while at sea.

Besides, he rationalizes, the luggage will be safe under the watchful eyes of Totino, Domino, and Papa John, the three *Royal Kansan* crew members who have to get off to make room for Jenny, Burson, and DeVille.

Jenny has never looked better. The sun, sea, and salt have turned her hair into a gorgeous California blond, her once pale skin is now taut, tanned, and creamy, her smile is radiant and constant.

She feels good.

Burson, for his part, does not regret the time away from other duties.

This is just the break I needed, he thinks.

Only DeVille seems less than satisfied with his present situation: a mere passenger on some other captain's ship; a captain himself with neither ship nor crew; a seventh-generation purebred pirate with no prospects.

With his way of life literally sunk, what's left to offer Jennifer Snow?

The following evening, the night before their anticipated arrival in the port of Fort Lauderdale, Coop comes across Jenny leaning over the rail, watching the ship's wake sparkle in the moonlight.

"It looks like fireflies," she observes softly. "Or fairies."

"Or diamonds," adds DeVille.

"Always the pirate," Jenny remarks.

"That's what I need to talk to you about," Cooper says. "I have to say goodbye."

"What?" Jenny responds, startled from her reverie.

"Captain Svenson has found me a captaincy on the *Royal Kansan*'s sister ship, the *Royal Nebraskan*. I sail tomorrow."

"I'll come with you," Jenny offers.

"No, Jenny," Cooper insists. "Not this time. Where I'm going, you can't follow. What I've got to do, you can't be any part of. Today, cruise ships are the real pirate ships, staffed with well-dressed pirates who fleece the old folks and honeymooners while plying them with fancy food and flattery and flashy casinos and plenty to drink. It's a nasty, ruthless business—not at all a proper life for a nice girl like you."

"But . . ." Jenny says hesitatingly, "what about us?"

"We'll always have Turtle Rock," Cooper replies. "You're the half on land. I'm the half at sea. Forever, a common bond."

"Right," Jenny agrees. "Until my mother got involved."

Cooper places his arms around the tanned young teen and gazes into her sea green eyes.

Far, far away, as the lovers enjoy their last embrace, the renegade reconditioned rock from Kansas-by-the-Sea is colliding with the fragile hulls of the *Lusitania,* the *Titanic,* the *Bismarck,* and the *Maine.*

"I'm no good at being noble," Cooper says quietly. "But it doesn't take much to see that the problems of a couple of little people don't amount to a hill of beans in this crazy world. Someday you'll understand that."

Jenny's eyes well up with tears.

Gently, Cooper places his palm on her cheek.

"Here's looking at you, kid," he says, before he disappears forever into the darkness.

A MILLION-DOLLAR TREASURE

COOP DEVILLE IS RIGHT about one thing. In its own coincidental way, the Ugiri-Tom statue of the loggerhead turtle turns out to be worth millions, now that it is suddenly famous—more famous, even, than the venerable red lighthouse on the Kansas-by-the-Sea inlet.

In very short order, the South Florida Loggerhead Turtle Rehabilitation Center becomes the most popular attraction on the South Florida coast, stimulating huge donations from the lonely, elderly widows and widowers of Palm Beach County, some of whom sell their stolen artwork and cancel costly Caribbean cruises in order to increase their contributions.

Years later, upon graduating from Florida Atlantic University, Burson is named executive director of the center. By this time, Jenny owns a number of thriving Vespa dealerships—six locations from Saint Augustine to Key West.

She and Burson have a daughter, Emma, to whom, on her sixteenth birthday, Jenny presents the family locket with the coil of hair inside.

Emma, by now well steeped in the family folklore, and

secretly proud of her mother's daredevil teenage adventures, decides to have a DNA test performed, a simple, inexpensive procedure available while you wait at ear-piercing kiosks in shopping malls.

What Emma learns is that her mother is a direct descendant of Edward Teach, also known as the notorious pirate Blackbeard. Had Jenny not been constantly changing her hair color in her early years, had she simply compared her natural hair with the contents of the locket and the hair of Coop DeVille, she might have suspected this herself.

No wonder she is such restless soul, so attracted to adventure. It's in her genes.

Jenny Snow and Cooper DeVille are cousins.

Distant cousins, to be sure, but not all that distant.

Not too distant to be kissing cousins.

"Dang!" says Emma when she is handed the long printout of scientific confirmation from the gum-chewing teenage girl at the mall. "You could knock me over with a spider!"

ABOUT THE AUTHOR

RICHARD W. JENNINGS is the "master of Middle-American whimsy" according to *Kirkus Reviews*. The *Horn Book* explains, "He writes about children who are witty, intelligent, articulate, and likeable," and adds, "His novels are laced with droll tongue-in-cheek observations, philosophical musings, and slight hints of absurdity." The author says his work "celebrates the custodians of optimism — kids — and is dedicated to every kid who ever felt different."

Since leaving the world of business in 1999, longtime Kansas resident Richard W. Jennings has published an impressive number of novels through the 150-year-old book publishing company Houghton Mifflin, Boston, under the guidance and imprint of Walter Lorraine.

Jennings's debut novel, *Orwell's Luck,* was launched to widespread critical acclaim in 2000, published in France as *La Chance De Ma Vie* in 2001, and released through Houghton Mifflin and Scholastic Books as a trade paperback in 2006.

This success was followed at roughly annual intervals by *The Great Whale of Kansas* (2001), *My Life of Crime* (2002), *Mystery in Mt. Mole* (2003), *Scribble* (2004), *Stink City* (2006), and *Ferret Island* (2007), praised by the professional media and found in schools and libraries throughout the United States.

Several of these works have been excerpted or serialized in the *Kansas City Star,* including *Orwell's Luck, Scribble, Stink City, Ferret Island,* and Jennings's most recent work, *The Pirates of Turtle Rock.*

Jennings is winner of two consecutive fellowships from the Kansas Arts Commission, and is the first novelist for young people to win the William Rockhill Nelson award for fiction from the Midwest Center for the Literary Arts. He shares his Kansas City–area home with three dachshunds, where he writes full-time.